The Coin Collector

The Coin Collector
A Nathan Perry Mystery

CAROL PREFLATISH

Cover design: Stephen Zimmer

Cover art in this book copyright © 2020 Stephen Zimmer & Seventh Star Press, LLC.

Editor: Stephen Zimmer

Published by Seventh Star Press, LLC.

ISBN Number: 978-1-7362781-2-3

Seventh Star Press

www.seventhstarpress.com

info@seventhstarpress.com

Publisher's Note:

The Coin Collector is a work of fiction. All names, characters, and places are the product of the author's imagination, used in fictitious manner. Any resemblances to actual persons, places, locales, events, etc. are purely coincidental.

Printed in the United States of America

First Edition

Acknowledgements

I want to give a big thanks to my family. During 2020, I lost both my husband and my brother, the pandemic hit, and I moved to a new city. If it hadn't been for the help that my whole family gave me, I don't know how I would have made it through it all. Thank you.

For my late husband.
He wouldn't read any of my romances, and never got
the opportunity to read my mysteries.
I love you, and miss you every day.

Chapter One

Detective Nathan Perry arrived to work at the Mystic Police Department early Wednesday morning. Anxious to see everyone, it was his first day back since his former girlfriend, Katherine, had given birth to their son, Simon. Nathan had spent the last thirty days with them at Katherine's home in Washington, D.C.

Walking down the hallway, he thought it was strange that no one was around. He unlocked the door to his office and stepped inside. Everything was just as he left it. Sitting at his desk, he placed a framed photo of Simon to his left and smiled.

Hearing something in the hallway, he got up to see if he could find someone. Again, the hall was empty. Now, he was getting concerned, and he went to the breakroom. Finding it empty too, he went to the Briefing Room and opened the door.

"Surprise!" All the officers and staff were there, waiting for him. A banner stretched across the wall that said, *"Congratulations, Dad!"*

"Wow, I had no idea about this. Thank you," Nathan said.

"Come in and tell us all about him, Dad," Hank McCoy said.

"You better have some pictures," Officer Gloria Wheeler said, giving Nathan a hug.

"Of course, I do." Nathan took his cell phone out of his pocket and pulled up the first of many photos and handed it to her.

"Oh Nathan, he's adorable," she said passing the phone around. The other female officers and staff went through the usual *oooo's* and *ahs*.

Suddenly, the room fell very quiet. Everyone was looking in the same direction. Nathan turned and saw Chief Cabot at the door. Gloria placed the phone back into Nathan's hand.

"Chief, thank you for coming to my party." As soon as he said party, Nathan knew it was the wrong thing to say.

The chief cleared his throat. Evidently, he was trying to decide what to say. "Congratulations on your son's birth, Perry. I, ah, I brought some cupcakes for everyone. They're in the breakroom."

The room remained quiet and no one moved a step. Nathan, as well as everyone else, was in complete shock at what the chief had done.

"Would you like to see a picture of him?" Nathan finally asked. He didn't wait for an answer and walked over, showing Chief Cabot one of the photos on his phone. "His name is Simon."

The chief looked at the phone. "He's a fine-looking boy." Then, he looked past Nathan. "Why aren't you people going after the cupcakes. You don't have all day to celebrate. There's work to do." The chief stepped out of the way as everyone rushed out of the briefing room to get a cupcake.

Nathan followed the chief out and saw him turn toward his office. "Aren't you going to join us?"

"No, my sugar level has been a little high lately. Enjoy them, and then back to work." He continued walking away.

"Just when I thought he'd mellowed a little over the last month," Nathan said to Hank and Gloria.

"It looks like he did mellow. He brought cupcakes to the party," Gloria said.

"The new mayor was elected while you were gone."

2

The Coin Collector

Hank said.

"It's a woman and I don't think the chief knows how to handle that yet," Gloria added.

"It's definitely going to be interesting watching that interaction," Nathan said.

***

The next morning, Nathan met Hank at the Witch's Brew Café for their usual to-go morning coffee, sitting next to him at the counter.

"You two have to do something about these kids and their pranks," owner Ginger Raines said.

Some things hadn't changed in the last month and Nathan saw that Ginger still wore her red hair spiked tall and stiff. He nodded his head in agreement.

"I've told the patrol officers to watch the place, but I'll say something to them again," Hank said.

"I'm telling you, I'm tired of cleaning raw eggs from my windows every morning. If the Mystic PD won't do something, I will."

"It's getting close to Halloween, and you know how things get around here this time of the year. The kids get mischievous and we get the overflow tourists from Salem," Nathan said.

"I don't care. Just remind the night shift to watch my place," she asked.

"I will, I promise," Nathan said.

Ginger stepped away from the counter to get their coffee.

"Her complaint's valid," Hank said. "Almost every morning when I stopped by for coffee, she or one of her workers is out cleaning the windows."

Ginger brought their cups of coffee. Nathan handed her a five-dollar bill, but she refused. "You know the police get their coffee free, and remind that to those patrol officers.

Maybe they'll come around more often to keep those kids away."

Before Nathan could respond, his cell phone rang. "Perry," he answered. He listened intently to the person on the other end of the call. "Officer McCoy is with me and we'll head right over." Nathan ended the call. "Thanks for the coffee, Ginger." He stood and looked at Hank. "We have a body." The two men headed out the door.

"Where?" Hank asked.

"The Mystic Inn. It looks like a possible murder. You drive in front, and I'll follow behind in my car," Nathan said.

When they arrived at The Mystic Inn, a female officer was waiting out front.

"Is that Officer Walker?" Nathan asked Hank, when they got out of their cars.

"Yes. The chief transferred a few female officers from administrative to patrol since the new mayor started," Hank said, as they approached Officer Walker.

"Cindy, what do we have?" Nathan asked.

"A housekeeper found a body about thirty minutes ago. No one has touched anything as far as I know." She led them inside as she talked.

When they reach the room, Nathan entered first, followed by Hank, to find a male body on the floor and a pool of blood soaked into the carpet. "Where's the housekeeper now?" Nathan asked.

"The manager took her to his office," the young officer said.

"Has anyone taken her statement?"

"Not yet. I wanted to secure the scene first," Officer Walker said.

Nathan turned to Hank, "Can you go take her statement?"

Suddenly, they heard a commotion in the hallway. Nathan, Hank, and Officer Walker stepped out to investigate and found another officer trying to keep two men from going into the room.

Nathan turned to Hank, "Go find the housekeeper." He then assisted the other officer. "Gentlemen, I'm Detective Perry. Can I help you?"

"Why are the police in Chuck's room?" one of the men asked, trying to look around Nathan and into the room.

Officer Walker took a step back and closed the door.

"Did something happen to Chuck?" the other man asked.

"Who are you two?" Nathan inquired.

"I'm Mike Metcalf and this is Tom Clark. We're friends of Chuck's."

Nathan took his notebook and pen out. "What's Chuck's last name?"

"Chuck Blanton," Metcalf said. "We're here for the coin convention."

"We're collectors," Clark added.

"Was Chuck a collector too?" Nathan asked. He wrote down Blanton's name.

"Yes. What happened?" Clark asked.

"And, this is Chuck's room?"

"Yes, it is."

"Someone was found dead in your friend's room," Nathan said.

"Was it Chuck?" Metcalf asked.

"An identity hasn't been made yet."

"Can we see if it's Chuck?" Clark asked, starting to step around Nathan.

Both Nathan and Officer Walker blocked the way. "No one is allowed in the room. I'm sorry," Nathan said.

Both men looked at each other, obviously knowing the body had to be their friend.

"Officer Walker, will you please take a statement from these men?" He then turned to Metcalf and Clark. "Could both of you come down to the police department this afternoon at about two-o'clock? I'd like to ask you both some more questions." He handed them one of his cards.

"We'll be there."

"Thanks."

Hank returned from the manager's office. He and Nathan stepped just inside the room, trying not to disturb the crime scene. "The maid was pretty shaken up. She said she came in and found him on the floor. She assured me she didn't touch anything, just ran out the door to get help."

"Did she go back inside later?"

"She said the manager came back with her to make sure it wasn't a dummy. He thought since it's close to Halloween, that someone might be playing a prank."

"Which it wasn't," Nathan said.

"Right. Once the manager saw it was a real body, they left the room and called us," Hank said.

"Did the maid see anyone hanging around the hallway?"

"No," Hank said. "You know the chief is going to want the State Police involved."

"Yeah, I know," Nathan said.

"What are you going to do?"

"I'm going to call Sam Denzinger."

"The state police detective?"

"Yes. He'll let me handle the investigation with their assistance, if needed."

"Are we going to need it?" Hank asked.

"It's too early to tell. We'll have Mallory collect the evidence and send it to the state police for analysis." He took out his cell phone and called Mallory Duncan, Mystic PD's only CSU technician, and asked her to come to the scene as soon as possible. Then, he called Denzinger, making an official request of the state police's assistance.

"Denzinger's Office."

"Sam, its Nathan Perry from Mystic."

"Well hello, Nathan. How's fatherhood?"

"It's different. I was calling because we've had a murder in Mystic and the chief is going to ask me for your assistance."

"You don't need my assistance," Denzinger said. "You solved that last murder just fine."

"I know, but Chief Cabot has a short memory."

"If you need anything, anything at all, you know I'm available."

"Thanks. I appreciate that."

"Detective Perry?" Officer Walker said.

Nathan ended his call with Denzinger. He looked over and saw the coroner standing in the hallway behind her. He stepped out of the room to greet the coroner. "Morning, Vince. How ya doing today?"

"Well, business is down at the funeral home, but looks like I might have a customer now," Vince Scanlon said, while placing plastic booties over his shoes so he could walk into the room. He then handed Nathan a pair.

"This one looks like a possible murder, so we just need for you to call the death. Can you wait until Mallory gets here to collect any evidence?" Nathan said, putting the booties on.

"Sure. You're going to want an autopsy, right?"

"I thought I would leave that decision up to you, but my guess would be yes."

As the two men walked over to the body, Scanlon put a pair of rubber gloves on and trying his best not to move the body too much, he knelt down to check for a pulse on the victim's neck. "No pulse, nor any respiration, and from the looks of the amount of blood soak into the carpet, I'd have to speculate he's been here for a while." Scanlon took out a thermometer and took the liver temperature. He stood back up and removed the gloves, placing them inside of a plastic zipper bag. "He's probably been dead for about six hours, making time of death around three a.m."

The two men walked back to the door where Scanlon had left his bag. He removed a leather-covered clipboard and started jotting down some notes. "Do you know the victim's name?"

"We haven't had an ID made yet, but we believe he's Chuck Blanton, from Boston," Nathan said.

"I'll wait around until Mallory gets here and finishes,

and then I'll take him to the funeral home and call the State Medical Examiner. They'll send someone to pick up the body. I'll send all the preliminary paperwork to your office as soon as I'm finished with it."

"Thanks, Vince. I appreciate that."

The two men stepped out into the hallway, which had now been cleared of sightseers. Hank was standing there talking to Officer's Walker and Stevens, who were stationed at the door.

"Officer Stevens, could you put crime scene tape over the door until Mallory Duncan arrives to collect evidence, and then Mr. Scanlon can take the body."

"Yes, sir."

"When they get here, call me, and don't let anyone in the room except Mallory or Scanlon."

"Yes, sir." The officer left to get the crime scene tape from his car, leaving Officer Walker to guard the door.

Nathan and Hank walked down the hallway. "Did you find out who's in charge of the convention?" Nathan asked.

"Yes. According to the hotel manager, the director is Alex Gold. She holds this convention in a different city in Massachusetts every year."

"Do you know where she is now?"

"Probably in the convention room."

"Let's go find her."

The two officers walked to the convention center that was a part of the hotel complex. At the doorway, they found someone checking convention ID's before allowing entrance.

"Can you tell me where to find Alex Gold?" Nathan showed the lady at the door his badge.

"She's somewhere inside."

"We need to see her."

The lady stepped aside, allowing them entrance into the room. "Try looking near the stage."

Inside the doorway, the two officers stopped to look around the room. Hundreds of tables filled the room, and it was packed with people.

"Your suspect list just got a lot bigger," Hank said.

"It sure did."

"That's Alex," the lady from the doorway said, pointing to the right side of the room.

Standing in front of the stage was a tall, slender woman. Her long, blonde hair fell below the shoulders of the black blazer she wore with the matching slacks.

"Let's talk to her," Nathan said, starting toward her with Hank following.

"Ms. Gold?" Nathan asked.

The blonde looked up from her paperwork. "Yes. Can I help you?"

Nathan showed her his badge. "Do you know Chuck Blanton?"

"Yes, I do. What about him?"

"Is there somewhere we can talk?"

"We can sit at that table," she suggested, motioning toward a table and chairs to the right of the stage. The three of them went to the table, with the men allowing Ms. Gold to sit first.

"Obviously, you know me, can you tell me who you are?" she asked.

"Of course, I'm Detective Perry of the Mystic Police Department, and this is Officer McCoy. We're need to speak to you about an incident that occurred in Chuck Blanton's room here at the hotel."

"Incident? What happened?"

"A body was found in Mr. Blanton's room," Hank said.

"Oh, my goodness," she gasped. "Was it Chuck?"

"We haven't had an official ID yet, but we have reason to believe it was. Have you seen Blanton today?" Nathan asked.

"No, I don't think I have."

"What can you tell us about Mr. Blanton?" Hank asked.

"Well, he's an avid collector of U.S. coins. He rarely misses any of my shows in the area."

"Did he set up a table to sell his coins here?" Nathan asked.

"Not a table, but instead he had a coin to sell in the auction." She thumbed through the papers on her clipboard. "Here it is, it's a rare Colonial coin."

"How rare?" Nathan asked.

"There's only been three others reported in existence. No one even knew there was a fourth coin until Chuck told everyone he'd obtained it."

"Is it real?" Hank asked.

"I don't know. Chuck never showed it to anyone, but he was going to sell it at the auction on Sunday."

"Don't you have to authenticate it for the auction?" Nathan asked.

"Yes, we were going to do that the night before the auction. Poor Chuck." She looked genuinely concerned.

"Thank you, Ms. Gold. We may be in touch later with more questions, and if you think of anything else, please give me a call." He handed her a card and the two men got up, leaving her at the table.

"Let's walk around a little before we leave. I want to see what we can find out," Nathan said.

He and Hank started walking around the convention hall and found that the news of what happened to Chuck had spread fast. They stopped at a few tables to ask if they knew anything about Chuck and left their cards.

After checking out the whole room, they found themselves back at the entrance. Nathan's phone rang. It was Officer Stevens reporting that Mallory had arrived to collect the evidence. He hung up the call and looked at Hank. "Mallory's here. Let's go back to the room."

When they returned to the room, Vince Scanlon met them at the door. "Mallory found a wallet in his pocket. The photo on the driver's license matches the deceased." He handed Nathan a plastic bag with the driver's license in it.

"We'll still need to confirm his identity with fingerprints, but at least it's a start," Nathan said. "Tell Mallory we're going back to the PD."

Nathan and Hank started down the hallway to the lobby. As soon as they walked through the door to the outside, they ran right into Dana Tyler, local newspaper reporter, Nathan's high school sweetheart, and occasional date.

"Good morning, Nathan, Hank," Dana said. "I heard there's some excitement going on inside." She turned and walked with them toward their cars.

"I heard the same thing," Nathan said.

"So, are you going to fill me in, or do I have to go inside and snoop myself to find out?"

"There's not much to tell. A body was found in one of the rooms."

"And? There has to be more to it than that," she said.

Nathan stopped and took a deep breath. "You know I can't go into details about an on-going investigation."

"Oh, so there is an investigation."

"Well, if there wasn't, I don't think I would be here," he said.

"Come on, you've got to give me more than a body was found in a room."

Just then, they walked past Mallory's CSU van. Dana looked at the van, and then at Nathan, "You still don't want to make a statement?"

Nathan rolled his eyes. "The victim was found in a pool of blood by one of the housekeepers. We're not sure of cause of death yet, or if it's even foul play, or an accident."

"Who was the victim?"

"No ID has been made yet, but we believe he was a collector from the coin convention being held here."

"Nathan, this could be big, really big. What are you going to do?" Dana asked.

"No comment," he replied.

"I'm asking off the record, as your friend."

"I'll handle it."

"You better be ready. I received a phone call from a television station in Boston before I left my office, and they're sending a crew down," she said.

"How did they find out about this so fast?" Hank asked.

"Technology, internet, social media, police scanners. News travels faster now than ever."

"Must be a slow news day," Nathan said.

Dana turned to go into the hotel, but before she walked away, she looked at Nathan. "How was your trip to see your son?"

"It was really great. Do you want to see a picture?"

"Of course, I do."

Nathan took out his cell phone and showed her a photo.

"He's beautiful, Nathan."

"Thanks. His name is Simon."

"That was your father's name."

"Yes. Katherine wanted to name him after Dad."

"That's great." She handed the phone back to him. "I better go get some statements from the convention for my article. Talk to you later."

Nathan felt as though things had changed between he and Dana. Sure, she was his high school sweetheart, and they had slept together once since he moved back to Mystic, but they had both agreed that neither wanted a relationship. Now, he wasn't sure if that was what she really wanted.

Back at the department, Nathan got a sandwich out of the vending machine and started to his office.

"Perry!" called Chief Cabot.

Nathan stopped dead in his tracks and did an about-face. "Yes, sir."

"What have you got on the body at the hotel?"

"Not much yet. Looks like a murder, but we won't know for sure until we get the M.E.'s report and that will take some time."

"Any idea on a motive?"

"The event organizer said the victim had a very

rare Colonial coin that he was going to auction off at the convention," Nathan said.

"How valuable?"

"Apparently very valuable, but she hadn't seen the coin yet. I'm hoping Mallory will find it when she goes over the room."

"Keep me updated," Chief Cabot said.

"I will." Nathan went to his office and sat down, finally able to eat his sandwich.

"Tuna fish? I could smell that all the way down the hallway," a female voice at the door said.

Nathan took a sniff of the sandwich. "Sorry." He placed it on his desk.

"What can I do for you, Gloria?"

"I heard about the murder."

"News travels fast," he said.

"Well, I do sit next to the dispatchers' room," she reminded him. "I just wanted to tell you that I'd be happy to help anytime you need something for the case."

"Thank you. There is something that I need."

"What?"

"I forgot to get myself some coffee with my sandwich." He flashed her a big smile, knowing she hated it when the officers asked her to get them a cup of coffee.

"The jokes on you, Nathaniel," she teased.

He hated hearing his birth name as much as she hated getting coffee. Gloria brought her arm around from behind the wall, and held out a Styrofoam cup of steaming coffee.

He laughed and just shook his head. "Thanks. There will be two men coming in later to see me for an interview about the victim. Their names are Metcalf and Clark. Will you let me know when they get here?"

"Yes, sir." She gave him a salute, and then headed back to the front.

The phone on his desk rang. "Detective Perry."

"Nathan, it's Vince Scanlon. I took the victim's body after

Mallory checked it and did a very preliminary check. It looks like a single gunshot wound."

"What about his personal effects? Do you know if Mallory found any coins in the room?"

"There was a case with several coins in it. Mallory took it to check for prints," the coroner told him. "The M.E.'s office from Boston should be here soon to pick up the body."

"Thanks, Vince. I appreciate you calling," Nathan said, before hanging up the phone.

Almost as soon as the receiver landed on the phone, the intercom buzzed. "Nathan, Mr. Metcalf and Mr. Clark are here to see you," Gloria said.

"Thanks. Would you take one of them to the interview room? I'll be there in a few minutes." Knowing he wasn't going to eat that sandwich today, he tossed it into the trash can.

Walking down the hallway, he passed the chief and Hank talking about last weekend's Patriots football game.

He interrupted their conversation. "I'm getting ready to interview one of the victim's friends, if either of you want to watch."

Hank and the chief went into the observation room, and Nathan entered the interview room. Inside, he nodded toward the mirror, meaning for Hank to turn the video recorder on. Michael Metcalf sat at the lone table in the room. Nathan took the seat with his back to the mirrored wall and a note pad in front of him on the table.

"Mr. Metcalf, I'm Detective Perry. I spoke with you at the hotel."

"I remember."

"How long were you friends with Chuck Blanton?"

"So, it was Chuck." He lowered his head.

"Yes, we believe so," Nathan said.

Metcalf looked back up at Nathan. "I've known -- knew Chuck since high school."

"You know his wife then."

"Sarah. Yes, I know her. In fact, I called her just a while

ago to tell her what happened."

Nathan was not happy to hear about the phone call, but would deal with that later. "How was their marriage?" Nathan asked.

"Solid, as far as I know. They've been married for about ten years."

"Any kids?"

"No, no kids."

Nathan made notes on the pad of paper. "Did they have money problems?"

"Who doesn't nowadays?" Metcalf answered.

Nathan looked at Metcalf.

"I'm not sure. Chuck never mentioned anything about having money problems."

"Did he have any enemies?"

"You mean enemies that would want to kill him?" Metcalf squirmed a little in his seat.

"Not necessarily. It could have been an accident."

"Was it?" Metcalf asked.

"I'm the one with the questions here. Let me ask you this, do you know anyone who would want to harm Chuck?"

Metcalf let out a deep breath. "Chuck was an arrogant son of a bitch. He was always bragging about how he had rare coins and then wouldn't show them to anyone. Hell, even his wife was fed up with all the money he spent buying coins."

"How much was he spending?" Nathan asked.

"I'm not sure."

"How do you know his wife was angry about his spending?"

Metcalf took a deep breath and let it out. "I was at their house one day when she received a delivery for him. It was a coin that he'd bought. When she saw the invoice, she started screaming at him and waving that invoice around. I left as soon as I could," Metcalf said.

"When was this?"

"About a month and a half ago, I think."

"How much did the coin cost?"

"I have no idea. He never mentioned the cost."

"Did you ask Chuck about the incident later?"

"No. It really wasn't any of my business."

Nathan had been jotting down notes during the interview. He finished writing something and closed the notebook. "I think that's all the questions I have for you now. If I think of anything else, I may give you a call."

"Sure, anything you need."

"Thank you." Nathan stood up and shook hands with Metcalf and then showed him back to the lobby, where Thomas Clark sat drinking a Coke, waiting his turn.

"Mr. Clark, if you will follow me," Nathan said.

He led the way back to the same interview and went over the same questions with Clark as he did with Metcalf. For the most part, the answers were similar to Metcalf's.

Thirty minutes later, they were finished, and he escorted Clark back to the lobby. Nathan thanked the men again for their cooperation and said goodbye to them.

He headed back to the interview room and met Hank and the chief by the door. Hank handed him the DVD of the interviews and the men stepped into the room to discuss what they had heard from the victim's friends.

"I want to go to Boston tomorrow and talk with Blanton's wife, and I would like Hank to go with me, if you can spare him? She could have some information about that coin Blanton was going to sell," Nathan said.

"Are you considering her a suspect?" the chief asked.

"Yes, at least for now."

"Very well, you two go talk to her tomorrow. What about those two men? Do you think they were involved?"

"You never know. I thought Hank could check on their alibi and see if that clears them," Nathan said.

"Have you brought in the state police yet?" Chief Cabot asked. "This is too big for our department to handle without help."

Nathan looked at Hank and read his expression as if to say, *I told you so.* "I called Sam Denzinger. He was busy, but said he'd be available."

"Good."

"We can handle this ourselves, you know," Nathan said. "We solved the murder on Mano Island without their help."

"You're right, but I'd still like for them to be involved," Chief Cabot said.

Suddenly, the men noticed Gloria standing at the door. "Excuse me, but I've been receiving several calls from television stations and newspapers about this murder. What am I supposed to tell them?"

"How did they find out about it so fast?" Chief Cabot asked.

"Apparently, it went out over social media, and all the media outlets are picking it up," she said.

"You better set up a place to hold a press conference," the chief said.

As the chief started to leave the room, Nathan said, "Maybe you should field the questions from the press."

He turned to Nathan. "You just said you could handle it, didn't you? Well, do it. Keep me informed of the progress." He left the room.

Gloria still stood by the door, impatiently tapping her foot on the floor with her arms crossed.

"There's civil court scheduled all day tomorrow, so the courtroom will be in use," Hank said.

"The weather is supposed to be nice tomorrow. We can pull the podium out the back door of the department and use the parking area for the media to set up," Nathan said. "How does tomorrow afternoon at three sound, Gloria?"

"I think that'll work," she replied.

"Will you also call Dana at the newspaper and see if she can send that information out to the media people and also put a sign on the front door about the press conference? Maybe that will keep the inside of the building from being overrun by reporters."

"What about our public information officer?" she asked.

"Damn, I forgot all about him. Brief him on what's going on and direct all calls to him. I'll email him a copy of my report," Nathan said.

"I'll get right on it," she replied, leaving the room.

He turned to Hank. "Be ready to leave from here tomorrow morning at seven o'clock. I also want to meet with the M.E. and with Sam Denzinger tomorrow too, and wear plain clothes. No need for a uniform tomorrow."

"I'll see you at seven." Hank left.

Chapter Two

Early the next morning, Nathan and Hank were on their way to Boston, arriving at Sarah Blanton's home around nine.

"Nice house," Hank said, looking at the two-story blue Colonial home with a small, covered porch in front.

"Yeah, pretty much an upper middle-class home." Nathan put the car into park and they got out.

They knocked on the front door and, to their surprise, a man answered.

"May I help you?" he asked.

"I'm Detective Nathan Perry from the Mystic Police Department and this is Officer Hank McCoy. We're here to see Sarah Blanton."

"Of course, please come in. I'm Bruce Gates, Mrs. Blanton's attorney." He led them to the living room where a woman was sitting on the couch. "Sarah, this is Detective Perry and Officer McCoy."

"How do you do," she said, not moving from the couch.

"I'm very sorry for your loss, ma'am," Nathan said.

"Thank you. Please sit down. Would you like some coffee? I just put a fresh pot on."

"No, thank you," Nathan said.

"No, ma'am," Hank agreed.

Nathan opened his leather folder to a clean notepad

inside and began asking questions. "Before I begin, we need to advise you of your rights."

"Is she being considered as a suspect?" the attorney asked.

"Everyone connected to Mr. Blanton is a suspect until I clear them."

"Why aren't you questioning her at the police department then?"

"I assume she's in mourning, and as such would be more comfortable being questioned here than having to drive all the way to Mystic," Nathan said.

"I'll answer their questions, Bruce," she said.

Nathan looked over at Hank, who took out a small card and read her the Miranda Warning. "Do you understand each of these rights I have explained to you? And having these rights in mind, do you wish to talk to us now?"

"Yes, I understand and will talk with you," she said.

"Mrs. Blanton, do you know of anyone who would want to do this to your husband?" Nathan asked.

"No, no one."

"Did he recently have any disagreements with any friends that you know of?"

"No."

"What about enemies? Was there anyone he didn't get along with?"

"Everyone got along with Chuck. He was always the life of the party," she said, wiping her eyes with a tissue.

Nathan jotted something down on the paper. "How were you two financially? Any problems?"

"No more than any other couple. He worked for the subway system in Boston. Not a high paying job, but along with my job, we were able to pay our bills."

"Where do you work, ma'am?" Hank asked.

"I work for an action house here in Boston."

Nathan continued writing some notes. "Tell me about his coin collecting. That must have put a dent in your household budget," Nathan said.

"He'd been collecting coins since he was a kid, and had compiled quite a large collection. If he found one that he wanted to buy, he would sell some of his other coins to get the money to buy the new one."

"How big was his collection?" Nathan asked.

"He has one whole room here in the house where he keeps his collection. Would you like to see it?"

"Yes, we would."

Mrs. Blanton led them to a room in the back of the house, next to the kitchen, and then opened the door.

Inside the windowless twelve-by-twelve-foot room were shelves containing albums, binders, and several boxes. A couple of file cabinets were next to a desk that had a work light clamped to it. Nathan stepped inside and over to the shelf where the boxes were. "May I?" he asked, indicating the boxes.

Mrs. Blanton looked at her attorney, who nodded in agreement. "Sure, go ahead," she said.

Nathan took the lids off of each box, finding coins in their protective cases inside.

"Chuck mainly collected coins, but he does have some old paper money that he keeps in the file cabinets.

"What about his most valuable coins? Where did he keep those?" Nathan asked.

Sarah pointed to a painting on the wall. "There's a fire-proof safe behind that painting."

Hank walked over and removed the painting, revealing a safe flush with the wall. "Do you know the combination?"

"No, I don't. Only Chuck knew it, I suppose. He never told it to me."

"What about birthdays, anniversaries, or special days?" Hank asked.

Sarah told him several dates, but none worked.

"We will need to look inside that safe. Would it be okay if the state police sent someone over to see if they could open it?" Nathan asked.

Sarah looked at her attorney.

"I think you should get a warrant before we can let you take a shot at that safe, and we want your guarantee that the safe will not be destroyed in the process of opening it," Gates said. "But, could you wait a few days to allow Sarah to see if she can find where Chuck may have written the combination down somewhere?"

"I think we can do that. It'll take a couple days to get the warrant," Nathan said. He turned to Sarah. "Did your husband keep an inventory of his collection?"

"I'm not sure."

"Mrs. Blanton, do you have any idea what the value is of your husband's coin collection?" Hank asked, looking up from the album of coins he held.

"He told me a few months ago that it was valued in the thousands."

"What about insurance? With a collection that valuable, wouldn't he have made sure it was insured? What insurance company do you use?" Nathan asked.

"I'm not sure. Chuck took care of all the household business," she said. Tears began rolling down her face.

"Could we possibly go back to the living room?" Mr. Gates suggested, putting his arm around Sarah.

As the attorney suggested, they all went back to the living room. Mrs. Blanton sat back on the couch and composed herself. "I apologize."

"There's no need to apologize. We understand your loss," Nathan said. "I do have one more question. At the convention, your husband claimed to have had a rare Colonial coin that he was going to auction off there. Do you know anything about that?"

"He told me about a coin like that, but never showed it to me," she said.

"Did he say how he came into possession of this coin?"

"He didn't say. I assumed he had sold several of his other

coins in order to get that one. He told me he was going to sell it through an auction house in Boston."

"An auction house?" Hank asked. He and Nathan looked at each other. "The one where you work?"

"I don't know. He never said which one.?"

"Had he ever sold any of his coins through your auction house?" Nathan asked.

"No, he hadn't. Why do you need to know if he sold any at the auction house?" she asked.

"Three people told us that your husband was going to auction off the coin at the convention this week, but no one saw the coin."

"That makes no sense," her attorney said. "He would get much more money for it going to an auction house. The houses I know about in the city allow international bidding via phone calls. The coin wasn't recovered with his effects at the hotel?"

"No," Nathan said. "We haven't recovered the coin. We don't even know if there was a coin, since no one saw it."

"When can I have my husband's body?" Sarah said. "I need to make the funeral arrangements."

"We're scheduled to meet with the Medical Examiner today. I will see what I can do to speed up the process," Nathan said. "I think we are finished here.

Nathan and Hank stood. Nathan shook hands with the attorney and then turned to Sarah. "If you think of anything else, please give me a call." He handed her his card.

Sarah nodded, wiping a tear from her eye.

The two officers got in their car and headed to their meeting with State Police Detective Sam Denzinger.

"Do you think she had anything to do with the murder?" Hank asked.

"I'm not sure. I want to see how stable they were financially. When we get back to Mystic, can you see about getting a warrant and check into that?"

"Sure."

"I also really want to see what's in that safe," Nathan said.

"I kind of wonder if she was telling the truth about not having the combination," Hank said.

"I know. I was thinking the same thing, but nothing we can do about that. It would take too long to get someone there to open it today."

Traffic was getting a little heavy with it being close to noon in the city. It took about forty-five minutes for the officers to reach the state police building and find Sam Denzinger in his office.

"Gentlemen, come in. Would either of you like some coffee?" Denzinger offered.

"No, thanks," Nathan said. Hank declined also, and both sat down in front of Denzinger's desk.

"Here's the preliminary autopsy report," Denzinger said.

Nathan opened the file and held it so Hank could read it too.

"Fibers around the bullet wound indicate the gun was fired through a pillow," Nathan said.

"That might explain why no one heard a gunshot," Hank said. "I don't remember seeing a damaged pillow in the room."

"He cleaned up." Nathan looked up from the file.

"That would be my guess," Denzinger said. "Was the television on when he was found?"

"The housekeeper didn't say anything about that, but I'll check back with her to see." Hank took out a small pad of paper and made a note.

"The M.E. should have the autopsy finished this afternoon. I'll get the report right to you."

"Blanton has a safe in his house where he keeps his coin collection. The wife said she doesn't know the combination. I'm going to get a warrant to check it, but I might need some help from your department getting it open," Nathan said.

"We have just the guy to help. Give me a call when you

get the warrant and I'll arrange things."

"One last thing, I have a press conference scheduled for three o'clock. Any way you can come down for that."

Denzinger started laughing. "Sounds like the police chief is still giving you a hard time."

"Not as bad as last time, but if you were there, it would be a good show of inter-agency cooperation. You wouldn't want to miss a photo op, would you?"

Denzinger shook his head. "I think it's more about saving your ass than a photo op. I can be there. It'll at least get me out of here early."

Nathan and Hank got up to leave. "Oh, Mrs. Blanton wanted to know when her husband's body will be released. She wants to get the funeral planned," Nathan said.

"She can probably have him tomorrow. I'll have the M.E. give her a call later and let her know for sure."

"Thanks. See you in a few hours."

"I'll be there," Denzinger replied. "Wait, I forgot to congratulate you on becoming a father."

"Thanks." Nathan showed him the photo from his phone.

"He's a great-looking kid. What's his name?"

"Simon." Nathan looked at the photo, smiling.

"It's going to be hard to be so far away from him," Denzinger pointed out.

"It already is. You have no idea how hard it was for me to leave him to come back to work."

"I can't wait to meet him."

"Thanks."

Back out in their car, Hank pulled out into the traffic. "I'm starved. How about you?" he asked.

"I could go for something to eat, but we really need to get back to Mystic. How do you feel about drive-thru fast food?" Nathan asked.

"That sounds fine to me. There's some places outside of town on the highway toward home."

"Thanks for driving back. I really need to make my notes

for the press conference while we drive back."

Forty minutes later, they entered the city limits of Mystic. Nathan looked at his watch. "Swing by my place so I can change into more presentable clothes,"

"Will we have time to run past my house so I can change into my uniform?" Hank asked.

"Sure."

At two-o'clock, they finally arrived at the police station. Lined up along the street in front of the two-story brick building were four television vans with satellite dishes on top. Local residents were beginning to crowd around the trucks.

"I can't believe this is so important that all this much press has shown up," Nathan said.

With the rear parking lot blocked off for the press conference, Nathan and Hank entered the building through the front door.

Cat-calls and whistles filled the hallway from his fellow officers as Nathan walked down the hall toward his office wearing his suit and tie.

"Very nice, Detective."

"Who died, Nathan?"

"Are you getting married?"

Nathan ignored them all and went straight into his office. Looking out his window, he could see the reporters and their cameramen setting up. He turned back around when he heard a knock at his door.

"I brought your phone messages," Gloria said.

"Thanks."

"Are you nervous?"

"Hell yes, I am. It's been a long time since I have had to talk in front of a group of people with cameras," he nodded toward the window.

"You'll do fine. Just talk to them like you would talk to the parents of a teenager you caught drinking."

"You think that will work?"

"I don't know, but what could it hurt? I asked Sergeant

Donnelly to send four officers out there to keep everyone under control, and to make sure the reporters don't go anywhere they shouldn't. There'll be more out there during your speech."

"Thanks, Gloria. You sure know how to take control of things," he said.

"What would you do without me?"

"Well, now that you mention that."

"Oh, oh, I think I spoke too soon. What do you need?"

"Two things. How quick can you type up my statement?" He handed her his notes.

She looked over the papers. "I can have this typed up in no time. What else?" she asked.

"I want you up there with me."

"What?"

"I want you next to me during the press conference."

"Why?"

"In the last day and a half, you have been a big help and I am going to need you even more before this case is solved. Will you stand with me up there?"

"Well, okay."

"Good. You won't have to say anything, just stand behind me, next to Hank."

"Oh my gosh, I must look like a mess. I need to go fix my hair and makeup!" She took his notes and ran out the door, nearly knocking Sam Denzinger over on the way out.

"Excuse me," Gloria said, rushing past him on her way out.

He looked at Nathan.

"I just told her I wanted her standing with me at the press conference," Nathan said. "Come in, Sam."

Denzinger sat down in front of Nathan's desk and put a brown envelope on the desk. "I thought you could use this."

Nathan looked through it. "Autopsy results."

"It's just a quick draft. That's all I could get out of the M.E. before I left town."

"It's a start," Nathan said. "Thanks."

"Why such a big crowd of media out there?"

Nathan held up one of the pink phone messages that Gloria had given him. "According to this message from our local newspaper reporter, Dana Tyler, word got out about the Colonial Era coin. She said several collectors are calling that coin priceless, which is interesting since his wife and his buddies said no one has seen it."

"Do you know anything about coin collecting?" Denzinger asked.

"Very little, but I plan on questioning the director of the coin convention a little more as soon as I can." Nathan swiveled his chair toward the window. "Well, I'll be."

"What is it?"

"See that blonde over there in the green dress?"

Denzinger stood up to look out the window. "Yeah."

"That's Alex Gold, the director of the convention."

"Interesting that she's here," Denzinger said.

"Even more interesting are those two guys leaning against that car over there." He nodded to the right side of the parking area. "They're the victim's buddies that I interviewed yesterday."

Hank stepped inside the doorway and knocked. "I hope I'm not interrupting."

"Come in," Nathan said.

"Glad to see you made it, Detective Denzinger." Hank turned to Nathan. "One of the officers told me that there are several people from the convention out there for the press conference."

"Maybe one of them is the murderer," Denzinger suggested.

"Hank, would you ask one of the officers to take the video camera out there and film the crowd as soon as I start talking. I want a record of everyone out there."

"Will do." Hank stepped back out.

Nathan looked at the watch. "It's almost show time."

"You ever done one of these before?"

"I've stood up during them, but never as the speaker," Nathan said.

"You'll be fine."

"Nathan, I have your statement." Gloria stepped into the office and handed him a copy to look over.

"It's perfect. Thanks." He looked up at her. "You look nice. Everyone will have their eyes on you and I won't have to worry about how I look."

Gloria blushed. "I also made several copies to pass out to the reporters after you're finished." She handed Denzinger a copy.

"You think of everything," Nathan said. "I guess we better get this over with."

He, Denzinger, and Gloria stepped out of the office and into the hallway heading to the back of the building. Hank followed them out. At the back door, they met Chief Cabot, who was waiting to join them outside. They all exchanged hellos.

Nathan took a deep breath, opened the door, and stepped outside. The group of officers followed him out onto the small concrete porch where the podium was set up with several microphones perched on top.

Looking out onto the crowd of people, Nathan heard the click of digital cameras and cameramen starting their video cameras. He put his notes on the podium.

He spotted Alex Gold in the shade along a row of trees bordering the parking lot. Metcalf and Thomas were now standing front and center. He also saw Dana Tyler to the left side of the large group of people.

"Good afternoon. I'm Nathan Perry, Detective with the Mystic Police Department. I have a statement to read, and then will take questions." He looked down at the paper Gloria typed. "Yesterday, at the Mystic Inn and Convention Center, the body of Charles Blanton, of Boston, was found dead in his room. He was shot with a semi-automatic handgun. He was in Mystic for the coin convention being held at the hotel. At this time, we have no specific suspects. The investigation is ongoing and anyone having any information about the shooting should call the Mystic Police Department at 978-555-0101. You do not have to give your name. Also, we'd like to see any photos or videos taken at the coin show. Please contact us at the same number and we'll make arrangements to obtain those photos. Now, I'll take questions?"

"Detective Perry, is the victim's wife a suspect?" one of the reporters asked.

"No one has been ruled out as of yet, but it is still early in the investigation."

"This is a rare crime to happen in Mystic, isn't it?'

"Mystic is not immune from something like this, but our crime rate is very low."

"Does the Mystic Police Department have enough experience and manpower to handle an investigation like this?" another reporter asked.

"I'm the only detective, but our department consists of many excellent and experienced officers, all of whom are working in one way or another on this case. We have asked the Massachusetts State Police for assistance also. To my left is Detective Sam Denzinger of the M.S.P. Their crime scene unit is assisting in evaluating the evidence from the scene and our coroner asked the Medical Examiner from Boston to conduct the autopsy."

"What is the name of your coroner?"

"Vince Scanlon is our coroner. He was unable to be here today," Nathan said.

"Detective Denzinger, have you determined a motive for the murder yet?"

Denzinger stepped forward. "I am only here to assist Detective Perry, who is the lead investigator. I'll refer to him for the answer." He stepped back behind Nathan.

"It's still too soon to speculate on a motive. We have a few things we are checking into and also have more witnesses to interview," Nathan said.

"Sir, do you think there is a connection with the coin convention?"

"That is one of many areas we're exploring."

"I have a question, Detective," a female voice said from the middle of the group. "I understand that the victim was here to auction off a very rare and valuable Colonial Era coin. Is there any truth to that, and if so, has that coin been recovered?"

Nathan recognized the blonde reporter as Robin Fisher. He had seen her picture as a reporter in *Boston Magazine*. "We're considering all possibilities. Thank you all for coming today. That's all the information I have right now. A copy of my earlier statement will be available for all the media at the front of the police department in a few minutes. Updates, as they come in, will be released to the media. I believe there will be someone at the front desk to collect your contact information for follow-up releases. Our public information officer, Gary Patterson, will forward any updates to you. Thank you."

Hank opened the back door to the building and the small group of officers went inside.

"You did great," Gloria said.

"It went well," Nathan said. "Can you go pass out those statements?"

"Certainly." She headed to Nathan's office to get the papers she had copied earlier.

"Gloria," Denzinger said, stopping the officer. "Watch what you say to the reporters. They'll throw questions at you while you are trying to hand out those statements. They'll try and confuse you in order to get a quote from you."

"Yes, sir. Thank you for the advice. I'll be careful."

"I'll be up front in a few minutes, Gloria," Chief Cabot said.

"That warrant should be ready for the Blanton's financial records. I'll go see about that," Hank said.

Nathan and Denzinger went into Nathan's office. Chief

Cabot followed them in. "Detective Denzinger, thank you for heading up this case."

"As I said outside, I'm only here to assist Nathan on the case."

"But you will be here to oversee things?"

"I'll be here as soon as possible upon a call from Nathan to discuss evidence and suspects, but this is his investigation."

The chief just stood there. "I see," he finally said. He started toward the door.

"Chief Cabot," Denzinger said, stopping the chief. "You'll be even more of a target for the reporters. Be careful with what you say."

The chief smirked and left. Nathan just shook his head.

"Did I get you into trouble?" Denzinger asked.

"No. It's the same old thing."

"I wouldn't worry about it. Maybe after this case, he'll realize you can handle it."

"That's assuming I can solve this case," Nathan said. "I'm going over to the convention center to interview Alex Gold, the director. Do you want to tag along?"

Denzinger looked at his watch. "I think I have time, but I'll follow you over in my car so I can leave to go home from there."

The men drove over to the Mystic Inn and Convention Center, showed their badges at the door, and were allowed in. The lady at the door told them where they could find Alex Gold, and sure enough, she was sitting there looking over some paperwork.

"Miss Gold?" Nathan said. "Is there somewhere we can talk in private?"

"Again? I'm rather busy right now, as you can see."

"We can do it here informally, or we can do it at the police station under your Miranda rights. You decide."

"Oh, all right. The hotel has given me a room to use as an office this week. We can go there." She got up and walked away, not bothering to look back to see if they were following.

On the way, they passed the victim's room, still with the yellow crime scene tape on it. Miss Gold slid her keycard into the slot to her office door, and after the green light came on, she opened it, and they went in.

Inside, there was a rectangular table with two chairs. A laptop computer sat on the table. In front of the table, a couch and chair sat with a coffee table in the middle. She sat in the chair, the men on the couch.

"Let's get this over with," she said. She lit herself a cigarette.

"This is Detective Denzinger from the State Police," Nathan said.

"I know who he is."

"That's right, you were at the press conference this afternoon. I guess you weren't too busy to attend that," Denzinger said.

"Things were slow here this afternoon."

"You sound kind of defensive. Any reason for that?" Nathan asked.

"Putting on one of these shows is stressful. I can only imagine what can happen out on the floor while sitting in here talking to you."

"We'll try not to keep you long." Nathan glanced over at Denzinger, who nodded back at him.

"Did you see Mr. Blanton here at the hotel before he was murdered?"

"Yes. I saw him during the day on Wednesday, when he was setting up his table."

"He had a table here?" Denzinger asked.

"Yes, but after his murder, we took it down and sent everything to his wife."

"You didn't think the police would want to look through all of his things?" Denzinger asked.

"I didn't want to be accused of losing any of the coins that he was selling."

"Why didn't you mention this when I spoke with you

yesterday?" Nathan asked.

"I didn't think about it." She took a draw from her cigarette and blew smoke in their direction.

"Do you recall if the Colonial coin was with his other coins at his table?"

"Are you kidding? He refused to show that coin to anyone. The other collectors weren't even sure he had it. They thought he was pulling a hoax."

"What did you think?" Denzinger asked.

"I spent weeks working with Blanton to get this auction coordinated. It would have been the biggest thing of the convention. I mailed out V.I.P. invitations to several big-time collectors specifically to attend this auction. Almost all of them were coming. After his murder, I had to scramble to contact them before they left to come here. No sense in having those collectors mad at me for an unnecessary trip."

"Would it be possible to get a list of those collectors that said they were coming?" Nathan asked.

"Yeah, with a warrant. I even hired extra security people from Boston to come down here to make sure nothing happened to that coin. There's no way I will be able to make up the money I'm losing over that."

"It seems you spent a lot of money on something you hadn't confirmed even existed," Denzinger said.

"This is a business where you take chances." She looked at her watch.

"Is there anything else that happened concerning Mr. Blanton that you haven't told us about?" Nathan asked.

She took another puff of her cigarette, blew out the smoke, and snuffed it out in a coffee cup sitting on the table. "I can't think of anything, except that he said his wife wasn't happy that he was going to sell the coin here. He said she thought he could get more for it if he sold it in Boston."

"Was she right?" Nathan asked.

"I don't know. Like I said, I had some big-time collectors coming." She lit another cigarette.

"The show ends tomorrow, is that right?"

"Yes. On Sunday, we open at noon and close at five.

"When is the auction?" Nathan asked.

"It's Sunday. I considered cancelling it, but I'd lose a lot of money from the other coins being sold," Miss Gold said.

"Will everyone be leaving right away tomorrow?"

"The collectors will have until eight to get their things out of the room. Most of them will leave as soon as they load up."

"When will you be leaving?"

"I'll be leaving on Sunday."

"Thank you for your time," Nathan said, as he and Denzinger got up from the couch. "If I need anything else, I'll contact you at your office in Boston. Oh, and this is a non-smoking room. Put it out."

The two officers left the room and walked down the hallway, stopping in front of the Blanton's room.

"Their rooms were pretty close," Nathan said.

"It might be worth checking to see how their relationship was. It sounded like she spent a lot of extra money on this auction. His wife said she wanted him to sell the coin at her auction house in Boston. What if he told Miss Gold he had changed his mind?" Denzinger said. The men started walked toward the hotel lobby. "She could have gotten pretty pissed off about it and confronted him about it. Things could have heated up, and she shot him."

"But, why would she have a gun with her in his room?"

"Maybe she took it to persuade him to change his mind?"

"We have no evidence, but it might be worth following up on. I'll ask Hank to come out here tomorrow and talk to some of the collectors and see if anyone knew what their relationship was like," Nathan said.

As they walked through the lobby and reached the front entrance, an attractive woman stopped them. "Excuse me, are you two the officers investigating the murder?"

"Yes, ma'am. Can we help you with something?" Nathan

asked, recognizing her.

"I hope so. I'm Robin Fisher from *Boston Magazine*."

"And, from the *Boston Globe* newspaper. I know who you are, Miss Fisher. I saw you at the press conference today."

"Please, call me Robin. I don't know anyone in town and saw you two walking through the lobby and was hoping you could join me for dinner."

"I'm afraid I will have to decline," Denzinger said. "I'm on my way home and if I don't get back soon, my wife will have my clothes on the front lawn. Nathan, call me tomorrow, if you learn anything new. Miss Fisher, maybe another time." Denzinger walked out the front door of the hotel to his car.

"Well, how about you, or do you have a wife to go home to also?" she asked.

"No, no wife. I suppose dinner wouldn't hurt, but I can't talk about the investigation, no quotes, and you cannot write about anything that is said at dinner in your column," Nathan said.

"Agreed. Where should we dine?"

"How about we go to the Hawthorne Restaurant next door?"

"What kind of restaurant is it?" she asked.

"It's an upscale restaurant. They have a variety of food, but their specialty is seafood. It's not as pricey as it sounds though."

"Sounds like the perfect place."

"After you," Nathan said, waving his arm toward the front entrance of the hotel.

The Hawthorne sat on the edge of the harbor in Mystic and just a short walk from the Mystic Inn. The last rays of the sunlight fell upon the water as they entered the restaurant.

"Nathan!" came a voice from behind the hostess station. "It's been forever since you've been here." The white-haired lady rushed over to give him a hug.

Nathan recognized the voice immediately. "Hello, Barbara. It's good to see you." He kissed her on the cheek.

"Have you got a good table for us tonight?"

"I sure do, honey. Follow me. Becky, I'm going to seat them at table fifteen," she told the hostess standing next to her. Barbara grabbed a couple of menus and started off. "Come right this way."

The restaurant was brightly lit with a huge chandelier hanging from the center of the room. Red carpet highlighted the floral wallpaper around the room. Barbara took them to the back corner of the restaurant and seated them at a secluded table next to a window overlooking the harbor. Table settings were already in place with a wine glass at each seating. Barbara motioned for one of the waiters to clear the other two place settings, which was quickly taken care of.

"My goodness, you do look nice tonight, Nathan."

"Thank you, Barbara. I didn't have time to change from that press conference this afternoon."

"That was such a terrible thing to happen to this town and that poor man. But, you know what's worse?" she asked.

"What's that?"

"All those reporters it's bringing to town."

Nathan glanced at Robin, who just smiled.

"Do you know what kind of bad things they will write about Mystic? The tourist traffic is slow enough with winter coming on, it's bound to be worse now."

"Barbara, I don't think I introduced you to my friend. Robin, this is Barbara Sutton, owner of this fine establishment. Barbara, this is Robin Fisher, she's a reporter for the *Boston Globe* and *Boston Magazine*," he said.

"Oh, my goodness! I am so sorry. I didn't mean---."

"It's fine. I understand. Don't worry about it," Robin said. "I promise when I write my story, I will put a positive slant on Mystic. I'll even see if I can work in a good word about your beautiful restaurant."

"Really? You would do that?" Barbara questioned.

"I would do that. Everyone I have met so far in Mystic has been wonderful." She smiled at Nathan.

A waiter came up to the table and handed Nathan and Robin each a menu.

"Phillip, please bring these two a bottle of 1996 Pouilly-Fumé wine, on the house," Barbara said.

"Yes, ma'am," the waiter replied, leaving to obey her order.

"Miss Sutton, you really don't need to do that," Robin said.

"Nonsense, and call me Barbara. I think the world of Nathan and it's the least I can do for you after the terrible things I said."

"I really wish you'd let me pay for it."

"Don't even try. She'll never let you. I have tried many times to do things for her, but she always one-ups me," Nathan said.

"Well, in that case, thank you for the wine. It's very gracious of you."

"You're welcome, honey. Enjoy your meal," Barbara said, patting Nathan on the shoulder before walking away.

"Thanks, Barbara," Nathan said.

"She seems like an interesting person," Robin said.

"She was my sister's best friend in high school and almost like another sister to me."

The waiter brought the bottle of wine for them and poured each a glass. "Are you ready to order?" he asked.

Nathan looked at Robin. "Yes, I'm ready. I've been craving lobster since I got to town, and a side salad to go with it. Thank you," she said.

"And, for you, sir?"

"I'll have the grilled Haddock with a baked potato," Nathan said, handing the waiter both of the menus.

"Thank you," the waiter said, leaving.

Robin took a sip of the wine. "This is delicious wine."

Nathan took a drink of his. "Yeah, it is good."

"It was really generous of Barbara to give us the wine. You do know how much a bottle of Pouilly-Fumé costs, don't you?"

"No. I usually drink a beer." He laughed.

"The last time I had a bottle of this wine, it was over two-hundred dollars a bottle," she said.

"That much? I guess I will really owe her now." Nathan took a drink. "How long have you been writing for the Globe?"

"For about six years. I started at the bottom, doing restaurant reviews and covering concerts, and worked my way up to feature stories."

"How did you get the job writing the column for the *Boston Magazine*?"

"That sort of happened by accident. One of their regular columnists was on medical leave and they asked me to fill in for a month. When the writer came back to work, they offered me a new column and I accepted."

"The newspaper or the magazine doesn't mind you working for both of them?"

"As long as my stories don't conflict, they're okay with it." She took another sip of wine.

"Are you originally from Boston?" he asked.

"No, I'm from a little town south of Boston called Avon, but I did go to Boston College. After graduating, I stayed in town."

She sat her glass down. "My turn. I bet you've lived in Mystic all your life, were the high school basketball star, and then went to college before coming back here to join the police department. How's that?"

"Some of it is close, some of it is completely off."

"So, tell me."

"I am from Mystic, but I was the quarterback of the football team, and we won the state championship my senior year. I could have gone to college on a football scholarship, but decided to join the army instead."

"Really? You were in the army? Fascinating."

"After the army, and a little stay in Washington, D.C., I was hired as the police detective here. I've actually only been back here for almost a year."

The waiter interrupted their conversation when he brought their food. "Can I get you anything else?"

"No, I think we have everything we need. Thank you," Nathan said.

The waiter turned and left.

"This looks delicious," Robin said, taking a bite of her lobster.

"Well, how is it?" Nathan asked.

She chewed and swallowed. "It's wonderful. I won't have any problem writing something good about this restaurant. How is your fish?"

He swallowed. "Really good. The food here always is."

"I suppose you really do have an idea of who did the murder, right?" she blurted out.

Nathan sat his fork down on his plate. "I told you, I can't answer any questions about the investigation. If that was your sole agenda for this evening, then you've wasted your time."

"Oh no, I didn't mean to do that. It was just a question. I wasn't fishing for answers."

"There are several people from town in here seeing us together. If I make a comment about the murder and you print it, they'll know it came from me, whether I said it or not."

"I understand. I'm sorry, but you know we could help each other."

"We could? How's that?" he asked.

"Did you know that witnesses, neighbors, and co-workers are much more forthcoming with answers to a reporter like me, than with the police?" She took a bite of her salad.

"You want to be my snitch?" he joked.

"Something like that." She smiled.

"But, there's a catch, right?"

"It's a win-win situation for us. I give you information for your investigation, and you just make sure I get any press releases before the rest of the media does."

He thought for a few seconds. "I think we might be able

to do that," he said.

The waiter approached their table. "Would either of you like some dessert this evening?"

"Nothing for me," Robin said.

"I think we'll pass this evening. Could you bring the check?" Nathan asked.

"Mrs. Sutton took care of the bill, sir."

"We can't let her do that. She gave us the wine, but not the dinner, too," Robin said.

"Yes, ma'am. She instructed me to not take any money from either of you. Enjoy your evening," he said.

"Tell Mrs. Sutton we said thank you," Nathan said. After the waiter left, Nathan placed a ten-dollar bill on the table for the tip.

"Are you ready to go, or would you like some coffee?" Nathan asked.

"I'm ready." She stood up. Nathan helped her on with her coat, and they walked out into the night air.

"Are you staying at the Mystic Inn?" he asked.

"No, they were full. I'm staying at the Harbor House hotel."

"That's not far from here. I'd be glad to walk you back there."

"Thank you. I'd like that."

"I can't get over how beautiful and peaceful it is here tonight. The lights on the boats in the marina give the water a golden glow. I've never seen any place like this."

"Not even the Boston Harbor?" he questioned.

"No, the lights of the city drown out the beauty."

They walked along the boardwalk for about fifteen minutes until they reached her hotel, and then entered the lobby.

"I've had a pleasant evening tonight, Miss Fisher."

"Miss Fisher? Why are you being so formal all of a sudden?"

He laughed. "I don't know." He looked at his watch. "I

should probably be going. I have a lot of work to do tomorrow."

"On Sunday?"

"I'm investigating a murder, remember?"

"My room is in the Alden Building and the Constitution Room there has complimentary sherry each night. Would you care for a nightcap?" she asked.

"I thought you wanted coffee."

"Sherry sounds so much better."

"Maybe just one."

Nathan accompanied her to the building directly behind the main building of the hotel. They walked into the Constitution Room, finding it partially full and with a fire roaring in the fireplace. On the opposite side of the room sat several glass decanters of sherry on a table with glasses.

Robin poured them both a glass, and they sat on the couch in front of the fireplace.

"I'm really not ready for the night to come to an end. How about you?" She kicked off her heels.

Chapter Three

"Good morning, Detective," the dispatcher said when Nathan stopped by the radio room to pick up his messages.

"Morning, Melinda. Is there any coffee in the break room?" He glanced through the stack of pink memo sheets.

"I personally started a fresh pot a little while ago. It should be ready by now. Long night?" she asked.

"Something like that." He went to his office, got his cup, and nearly spilled yesterday's leftover coffee that was still inside it. After rinsing it out in the break room, he refilled it with fresh coffee, and immediately took a needed drink.

"Did you work all night?" Hank asked, standing at the doorway behind him.

Nathan considered telling him about his dinner date last night, but thought it best to keep that to himself for now. "Do I look that bad?"

"You look like you haven't had much sleep."

"I was up late, and then didn't sleep very well. What are you doing here on a Sunday?"

Hank poured himself some coffee. "I figured you'd be here today and wanted to fill you in on what I found out about the Blanton's financial records."

The men walked back to Nathan's office and sat down. Hank opened up a file. "Their credit score is pretty decent.

They're making a house payment, a car payment, and owe on two credit cards. They also have a loan on a computer purchase about two months ago. Basically, they're like everyone else, and live paycheck to paycheck."

"What about their bank accounts?"

"They have a joint checking and two savings accounts. One of the savings is in both of their names, but the other is in his wife's name only, and at a different bank."

"That's interesting. I wonder if Blanton knew about his wife's other account. What are the balances?"

Hank checked through the file. "Their checking has around two-hundred dollars in it, the joint savings about four-hundred and fifty, but her savings has eighteen-hundred dollars in it."

"More interesting."

"The bank record shows a couple automatic withdrawals from insurance companies coming out of their checking. I'll call tomorrow after their offices open and see if one of them might be a homeowner's policy that might cover the stolen coin."

"Good. Maybe they'll have an inventory on his collection in their records," Nathan said.

"That's what I am hoping for. Are you going to the coin auction today?"

"Yes. I'm anxious to see if Alex Gold mentions Blanton and his coin."

Hank handed a document to Nathan. "Here's the warrant you wanted for the list of auction bidders."

"Thanks. I know it's your day off, but want to go with me?"

"I better not. My wife would kill me if I worked on my day off. We plan on enjoying the day watching the Patriots' game."

"I'm praying I get home by halftime. Enjoy the game," Nathan said.

"Thanks. Enjoy the auction." Hank got up and left.

Nathan returned what phone calls he could on a Sunday and finished up some paperwork. He checked his watch, then decided to get a little lunch before going to the auction. It was a nice October day, so he decided to walk.

Heading up the hallway, he told the officer on duty at the counter that he was going to Ginger's for lunch. A short walk from the police department, Nathan entered the front door of the Witch's Brew, and took a seat at one of the tables.

Ginger walked over. "How are you on this fine October day?"

"Unfortunately, I'm working today."

"Me too," she laughed.

The dinging of the bell on the door announced another customer. This one headed straight for Nathan's table.

Dana Tyer sat down across the table from Nathan. Her long brown hair was wavy today, and her brown eyes sparkled as much as they always did. She was well-dressed for a Sunday. "Are you working today too?" Nathan asked.

"Yes, and no. I just got out of church, but am meeting someone for coffee later to do an interview for the newspaper.

"Can I get you two anything?" Ginger asked Dana.

"Just a small salad with Ranch dressing for me and some iced tea," Dana said.

"I'll take whatever your special is today and a Coke," Nathan said.

Ginger left with their orders.

"I thought you would have called me when you got home from seeing your son," Dana said.

Nathan was a little taken aback. "It was late when I got home, and I had to be at work the next morning. I saw you at the hotel Friday. You shouldn't be so surprised that I was home."

"It's fine. I'm sorry I brought it up."

A waitress brought their drinks and then left.

"Dana, is something wrong?" Nathan asked.

"No, it's nothing. It's just me." She put a straw in her tea and took a sip.

"I'm sorry I didn't call you, but it was late, I didn't want to wake you."

"It's okay, really it is."

"Let me make it up to you. How about I take you to dinner tonight?"

She took another sip of her drink. "Tonight's not good. I'm looking forward to a hot bath and a good book before going to bed."

"I could probably help with both of those," he suggested, winking at her.

"I don't think that's a good idea."

Ginger approached the table with their food. "Here you go. Salad for you, and a turkey melt with fries for you, Detective."

"Thank you, Ginger," Dana replied.

"Yeah, thanks," Nathan added.

Ginger left without saying another word.

"Why wouldn't that be a good idea?" Nathan asked.

Dana poured the dressing on her salad, but wouldn't look up. "You have other responsibilities now. You have a family in D.C. waiting for you."

"Waiting for me? What are you talking about? Just because I have a son now doesn't mean things have changed between us."

"I think we need to just remain friends, you know, without benefits. Just friends." She finally looked up.

"I don't understand. Me having a son shouldn't make any difference."

Dana looked at her watch. "Look at the time, I've got to go." She looked back to the counter. "Ginger, can you bring me a box for this salad?"

When she brought the foam container, Dana quickly poured her salad in and closed the lid. "I have to go." She left some money on the table, and got up to leave.

Ginger sat down in Dana's spot. "She's hurt, you know."

"Hurt how?"

"You have a son with another woman. It's a connection she doesn't have with you now."

"But that actually happened before I moved back here."

"It doesn't matter."

"Damn. I'll never understand women," he said.

"That's the way we like it." Ginger laughed as she walked back to the counter.

Nathan finished his lunch and left for the coin convention. When he walked into the hotel, he saw the manager at the front counter and approached.

"Hello, Detective Perry. How can I help you today?"

"Does Alex Gold have a room here, other than the one she uses for an office?"

"Yes, she does."

"Can you tell me the room number?" he asked.

"It's against policy for us to give out a room number. I'm sure you understand."

"If you recall, you had a murder here this week that I'm investigating. I'd hate to make it known that you weren't cooperating with me. Do you really want to hamper that investigation?"

The manager thought for a few seconds and then typed something on his computer. "She's in room 103. It's down the hall on the left." He gestured toward a hallway on the other side of the lobby.

"Thank you." He turned and headed toward the hallway, found room 103, and knocked on the door. After a couple tries and no one answering, he went to the convention hall.

He flashed his badge to the worker at the doorway and was allowed into the large room full of people. He walked around looking for Alex Gold but didn't find her. Finally, he stopped a staff member and showed his badge. "I'm looking for Alex Gold."

"She's in the auction room. It's almost time for it to start," the young man said, pointing toward a doorway leading off from the convention hall.

Nathan headed that way, and he was handed a program when he entered the room. Almost all of the seats were filled, but he noticed an empty seat next to Robin Fisher and made his way down the row to sit next to her. She smiled at him.

"You weren't saving this seat for another reporter, were you?" he asked.

"No, not at all."

"What are you doing here?"

"Same as you." She opened her program and showed him the listing for the coin that Blanton was supposed to sell.

Alex Gold was at the front of the room and stepped up to the microphone. "I want to welcome everyone to our action today. I do have a few announcements to make before I turn this over to our auctioneer." She went over a few changes in the program for coins that had been withdrawn from the auction. She hesitated before continuing. "As most of you know, we had an unfortunate event happen earlier this week. Collector Chuck Blanton passed away here at the hotel. Chuck had advertised that his Brasher Doubloon coin was to be auctioned off today. Due to his death, his family has chosen to withdraw the Colonial coin from the auction today, until such time that his estate can be settled."

Mumbles echoed throughout the room. Miss Gold continued. "Let me apologize to those of you who came specifically for this coin. I tried to contact everyone interested in it, but many of you had already departed for the auction."

Two gentlemen from the middle of the room stood and walked out. Nathan followed, and he found them standing not far from the door, talking to each other. He joined their conversation. "How much do you think that coin of Blanton's would have brought at the auction?" he asked.

"It's anyone's guess. I would think it could have brought well into the thousands," one of the men said.

At that moment, Robin Fisher walked up. "Gentlemen, I'm Robin Fisher, reporter from the *Boston Globe*. Were you here to bid on the Doubloon today?"

"Yes, we were interested in it," the other man said.

"I'm sure Detective Perry here would love to know just how interested in it you were."

"Detective? You didn't say you were with the police," the first man said.

"I just didn't get to it yet. I do have some questions for you, if you wouldn't mind answering them," Nathan said.

"We have nothing to say," the second man said and both of them walked away.

Robin started to follow them. "Gentlemen, if I could have a word with you."

Nathan grabbed her arm and pulled her back. "You need to leave the questioning to me."

She looked at her arm where Nathan still held her. "Seriously, are you going to run me out of town too?"

He let go. "This isn't one of your investigative stories. We're talking about a murder here. Leave the investigating to me."

"I have every right to talk to anyone I please for my story. Freedom of the press, remember?"

Nathan laughed. "Do you realize how dangerous it is to be asking questions about a murder?"

"Not the way I do it. You better get back to your auction, you might just miss something in there." She turned and walked away.

She was right about one thing. He needed to go back to the auction so he could talk to Alex Gold. He went back into the room and took his seat again, waiting for the auction to finish.

The auctioneer stood at the front of the room. "I have a bid of two-hundred dollars, do I hear two-fifty?" The auctioneer gazed around the room. "No more bids? Sold for two-hundred dollars." He pounded the gavel. "That completes today's auction. Thank you for coming."

The crowd started to file out of the room, all except the

bidders that won their auctions. They went to the table where Alex Gold sat to pay for the purchases. After processing their payments, she gave them their merchandise and each one left. Once everyone was gone, Nathan approached the table. "Profitable day?"

"It was," she said. "The auction alone will pay all of the expenses for the convention.

"And, you take a cut of the money?"

"I take a cut and so does the auctioneer." She logged off from the computer she was working on. "If Blanton's coin would have been up for sale, I could have made a lot more. Tell me, after visiting the convention, and now the auction, have you become interested in collecting?"

He ignored the question. "I'm going to need a list of people who intended on bidding on Blanton's coin, including the ones that didn't show up, or were going to bid online, or via a phone call."

"I can't give you my client list. You'll need a warrant to get that." She put her computer into her bag and stood.

"Can you promise me that by the time I get a warrant that the list won't be destroyed or accidently deleted from your computer?" he asked.

"I can't promise that. Shit happens, you know." She walked past him toward the door.

"I figured as much, that's why I brought a warrant with me."

She stopped, and turned back to him. He handed her the warrant. "Shall we go someplace where you can print a copy for me?"

"My lawyer will need to look this over, and he's in Boston."

He handed her his phone. "Call him."

She let out a deep breath. "All right, I'll give you the list, but my clients are not going to be happy about this." Alex pulled a sheet of paper from her bag and handed it to Nathan.

"Thank you. I'll make sure to mention I had a warrant to

get their names."

"Where do you get your auctioneer from?" he asked.

She took the program out of his hand and opened it to the last page, pointing to the line at the bottom. "My auctioneers are always from Harris' Auction House in Boston."

"Since the convention is over today, will you be leaving today also?"

"I'll be checking out tomorrow."

"I may need to contact you for further questioning."

She reached into her back and handed him a card. "You can contact me at my office."

"Thank you." Nathan turned and left the room. Before leaving the convention, he decided to take one more walk around the vendor hall. Many of the vendors had already started taking down their displays, but a few remained. Down the first aisle, he spotted Blanton's friends Michael Metcalf and Tom Clark packing away their table. "Hello, gentlemen. Have you had a profitable event?"

"Good afternoon, Detective. We've probably broken even," Clark said.

"Have you caught Chuck's killer yet?" Metcalf asked.

"We're still working on it. I didn't see you in the auction room. Were you not interested in that?"

"Without Chuck's coin in the auction, it wouldn't have been very interesting to us."

"Do you know anyone who was interested in buying the coin?"

"I don't know any names, but Chuck mentioned a few weeks ago that he had two people that wanted to buy from him outright," Metcalf said.

"How did he come into possession of the coin? He surely couldn't have afforded to buy it."

"That's what we wanted to know. A few collectors had doubts that he even had the coin, since no one had seen it," Clark said.

"You aren't the first to tell me that. Thank you for your

help, and I'm sorry about Mr. Blanton."

"Thanks. We're going to miss him"

Nathan walked away, but before leaving the room, he stopped by one of the vendor's tables and bought a book about coin collecting. As he walked to his car, he checked his watch and saw that he could probably get home in time to catch the last half of the football game.

He turned onto Golden Hollow Road and proceeded toward his home. A half mile down he saw an unfamiliar car parked in his driveway. He walked toward his front door with his hand behind his back on his holstered gun.

Gently, he tried to turn the doorknob, but it was still locked. He decided to walk around to the back deck and look through the glass doors. Slowly, he made his way around the house and peered around the corner, spotting Robin Fisher standing on his deck. He relaxed and stepped onto the deck. "It's kind of cold out here."

"It's not too bad as long as you're in the sunlight," she answered.

"What are you doing here?"

"I wanted to watch the Patriots' game with you."

Nathan laughed. "You could have called me." He unlocked the glass door and they stepped inside. "Would you like some coffee to warm up?"

"Actually, some hot cocoa sounds better."

"I don't think I have any," he said.

"If you have some baking cocoa, I can make some mocha coffee. That would be just as good," she offered.

"I doubt I have any of that either. I'm afraid the only thing I have is coffee, beer, or soda."

"I'll take a beer."

Nathan opened the refrigerator and got beers for them both.

"Have you eaten yet?" she asked.

"I have, but could eat again." He laughed. "I don't think I have anything to fix." He looked back in the refrigerator.

Robin peered over his shoulder. "You really are a bachelor, aren't you?"

"Card-carrying member." He raised his hand to swear.

"How about I order a pizza?"

"That sounds perfect. There's a menu for Hocus Pocus Pizza in the drawer to the left of the refrigerator. They'll be the quickest to deliver. I'm going to start a fire in the fireplace."

Nathan went into the living room and started working on the fire. Robin came in a few minutes later. "The pizza's ordered," she said. She grabbed the remote control and turned on the TV.

He looked up at her as she scanned the stations for the game. Her skin-tight leggings showed her very toned legs; the same legs he remembered wrapped around him in her hotel room last night. Quickly, he shook that memory from his head. He didn't need that right now. "Why did you come out here to watch the game? You could have gone to the bar at your hotel for that."

She found the game and sat down on the couch. Kicking her shoes off, she pulled her legs up under her. "I already checked out, and it's more fun to watch it with someone you know."

"I suppose you're right about that. I think the fire's going now." Nathan joined her on the couch. "Looks like the Pats are ahead at halftime."

Robin walked over to the fire to warm herself. She picked up the framed photo from the mantle. "Who's the little one?"

"That's my son, Simon."

"How old is he?"

"A little over a month old."

She quickly replaced the photo and turned to him. "Are you married?"

He could see the wheels turning in her head, thinking he had cheated on his wife with her. "No, I'm not married. Simon's mother is my former girlfriend. When we split, she didn't know she was pregnant. She lives in D.C. and I live here.

We're not involved anymore, except for loving our son."

"That's nice." She returned to the couch and sat down. "Let's talk about the murder."

Nathan took a drink of his beer. "You know I can't talk about that."

"What if I did the talking, and you just listened?"

"Intriguing. Has my snitch come through with something?"

"Possibly, but a snitch usually gets something in return for information." She moved a little closer to him.

"You're getting free pizza and beer," he joked.

"I used my credit card for the pizza."

"Good point. Didn't I pre-pay for any information last night?"

"Okay, I give up." She scooted back to her spot on the couch. "Blanton's wife had an affair."

Nathan sat up. "Really? Who with?"

"The only thing I could find out was that it was probably with someone Blanton knew. My source said she ended it when Blanton found out."

"Who is your source?"

"You know I can't tell you that anymore than you can discuss your investigation with me."

"You're right. This is something that could really help with the investigation. Thank you. I definitely owe you a dinner for that."

The doorbell announced a visitor. "That's probably the pizza. I'll get it," Robin said. She got up and left the room.

With this new information, it definitely put Blanton's wife at the top of his list of suspects. He'd have to question her again.

Robin walked back into the room. "Here's the pizza." She placed it on the coffeetable.

"I'll get some plates. Do you want another beer?" Nathan asked.

"Yes, please."

After the game was over, Nathan and Robin took the plates and beer cans into the kitchen. "I'll take care of the rest of the trash later," Nathan said.

"Are you sure? I don't mind helping to clean up."

"I'm sure. It was nice having someone to watch the football game with." He put the empty cans in the garbage.

"I really need to get on the road back to Boston." Robin walked over and put on her coat.

"You're going back already?"

"I have to be at work tomorrow, and I need to get on the road before it gets too dark." She put her scarf around her neck.

"I should have realized that."

"We should go to a Patriots' game sometime." She stopped what she was doing and stood smiling at him.

"I'm sure the all the games are sold out."

Robin put her gloves on and picked up her purse and phone, and started walking toward the front door. "The *Globe* has a suite, and I can get us tickets for it anytime."

"That sounds like fun." He stopped her at his door. "Would you mind if I called you the next time I'm in Boston to have dinner together?"

"I'd be mad, if you didn't." She gave him a peck on the cheek and then was out the door.

Chapter Four

The first thing Nathan did when he got to work Monday morning was call Sarah Blanton to ask her to come in for another interview that afternoon. She agreed. He sat at his desk, working on some reports while munching on the doughnuts he picked up on his way to work. His desk phone rang. "Perry."

"Perry, Chief Cabot here. The mayor wants to meet with us. Be ready in five minutes to drive me over there." The chief hung up before Nathan could even respond.

He popped the last of his doughnut into his mouth and took a drink of coffee before getting up. He then stood at the elevator, waiting for it to open.

The chief stepped off with a surprised look on his face. "I didn't expect you to be waiting here."

"You said be ready in five minutes."

"I did, but--" He stopped in mid-sentence. "Come on, let's go."

They walked out and got into Nathan's assigned car, before heading to the Town Hall. "I'm anxious to meet the new mayor. What's she like?" Nathan asked.

"She cares about the town," is all he said.

"That's important for a mayor." Nathan wondered what the chief really thought about the mayor, knowing he didn't like women in power positons.

It wasn't a long drive to the Town Hall, and they arrived in no time. The mayor's office was on the top floor. They stepped off the elevator in front of her office.

The new mayor had the same secretary as the old mayor. "Hello, Chief Cabot. The mayor is waiting to see you. Let me just let her know you're here." She picked up the phone receiver and pushed a couple buttons. "Chief Cabot is here to see you." She replaced the receiver. "You can go right in." The secretary gave Nathan a smile when he passed, and he winked in return.

They entered the mayor's office, and she stood behind her desk. "Gentlemen, please come in."

"Mayor Cranston, this is Detective Nathan Perry," the chief said.

Nathan was happy to finally meet the new mayor. While he had been in Washington with Katherine and Simon, Jennifer Cranston had won a special election after the arrest of the previous mayor, Robert Newcomb, for murder. She was younger than he expected, probably early thirties was his guess. She was tall and slender, with her long brown hair falling below her shoulders.

"I've been looking forward to meeting you, Detective."

"As I, you," he said.

"Please gentlemen, sit down." They all took a seat. "Paul, I've been looking over the crime reports and am pleased with what I'm seeing. For the most part, the overall rate seems to be going down, but the trend also shows the rate for shoplifting going up."

"That seems to happen every year during tourist season," the chief said. "Once Halloween is over and the tourists leave, it should decrease."

The mayor nodded and looked down at the papers on her desk. "Do you think there's anything we can do about that for next year?"

"Maybe better education for the shopkeepers. It really relies upon them and the security they have in their stores."

"Perhaps over the winter, we could set up something with the Chamber of Commerce to give a presentation to the store owners about security," she suggested.

"That sounds like a good idea."

Nathan was trying to read the mayor. She was all business and didn't jump right into the financial aspect of tourism first thing.

"Detective Perry, what's your impression of overall crime in Mystic?" she asked.

"Overall, I think we're doing a fine job. Of course, as with every police department, we could always use more officers, but we do the best with what we have."

"I see." She picked up the newspaper from her desk. "What about the murder at the Mystic Inn? How is the investigation going?"

"It was a terrible thing, but we're working on it," he replied.

"The manager of the hotel called me yesterday, and was very upset that things aren't moving faster. He believes his hotel is losing business because of it. He said that several people have cancelled their reservations."

Before Nathan could respond, Chief Cabot jumped in. "Most people don't realize how long it takes to complete an investigation. They're used to seeing a murder solved on television in an hour. Police work takes longer than that."

Nathan was impressed with the chief's response. "The chief is right. I'm still interviewing people, and am waiting on some reports from the State Police Crime Lab."

"So, what do I tell the hotel manager?"

"Tell him to call me, if he complains again," Nathan said.

"I will do just that."

The rest of the meeting was the mayor discussing the upcoming Halloween festival with the chief. Nathan just sat and listened, wishing he could be back at his office working on his interview questions for Sarah Blanton.

"Gentemen, thank you for coming in today." The mayor

stood, as did Chief Cabot and Nathan. "Detective Perry, good luck on your investigation."

"Thank you, Ma'am."

"Paul, could we schedule weekly meetings so I can keep updated on what is going on with the police department?"

"Yes, we can. I'd like to do that," he replied.

"Good. Thank you, again." She walked them to her door.

The two men left her office and made their way back to the car. "Thank God, that's over," the chief blurted out, once in the car. "And, she wants weekly meetings!"

"You acted like you wanted the meetings," Nathan said.

"She's my boss. What was I supposed to say?"

Nathan hid his laughter and drove them back to the police department.

Later that afternoon, Nathan was researching rare coins on the internet when his intercom buzzed. "Yes."

"Nathan, Mrs. Blanton and her attorney, Mr. Gates, are here to see you," Gloria said.

"Thanks. I'll be with them in a few minutes."

He got up and checked to see if Interrogation Room One was available and then went to the lobby. "Mrs. Blanton, won't you please come with me?" He led her and Gates to the room. "Please sit down."

Mrs. Blanton and her attorney sat on one side of the room, with Nathan sitting with his back to the mirrored wall. "Thank you again for coming in today. I have a few more questions for you."

"You couldn't have done this over the phone?" Gates asked.

"I prefered to do this in person, as it's a little more official than when we last met."

"I don't understand." Mrs. Blanton looked at her attorney.

Gates touched her arm to quiet her. "Would you please explain that, Detective?"

"Some new information has come to me that I have further questions about. Unfortunately, before I ask them, I need to remind you of your rights from the other day."

"What? Bruce, what is he talking about?"

"Detective, is Sarah a suspect now?"

"You know that a spouse is always a suspect until we can rule her out."

"Go ahead," Gates said, giving Mrs. Blanton a reassuring look.

"I'll start with the easy questions. The state police said they were able to open your husband's safe and that coin wasn't there. Were you able to locate it anywhere else?"

"No."

"You haven't found it anywhere?"

"No, I haven't."

"How did you feel about your husband spending so much money purchasing coins?"

She looked at her attorney, who said she could answer. "It was okay with me, as long as we could still pay the household bills."

"Interesting, because I understand that you opened one of his deliveries and saw the cost on the invoice, which caused you to become enraged with him."

"I-ah-well, that was just once, and he explained that he had sold some coins to get the money to buy that one. It was all a misunderstanding."

"Why do you have a separate savings account from the one you have with your husband, and at a different bank?"

"You're looking into my bank accounts? Bruce, why is he doing this?"

"Detective, before you continue, please understand that I am advising my client to not answer any more of your questions until we know what is going on," Gates said.

"Of course, information has developed that Mrs. Blanton had an extra marital affair with someone, and Chuck found out about it." Nathan looked at Mrs. Blanton, whose skin color had turned white as a ghost.

"Where did you get this information?" Gates asked.

"You know I can't divulge a confidential informant. Now that you know the basis for my questioning, Mrs, Blanton, is this information true?"

She looked at her attorney.

"Could I have a moment to speak to my client alone?" Gates asked.

"Certainly. I'll be right outside." Nathan left the room and waited in the hallway.

About ten minutes later, the door opened and Gates said they were finished. Nathan went back in and sat down.

"Mrs. Blanton will only answer the questions that I allow her to answer," Gates said.

"Very well.

"Mrs. Blanton, first tell me about your savings account?" Nathan asked.

"My husband never let me have any of my own money. Everything always went into our joint accounts to pay the bills, and for him to buy coins. I couldn't even have money for nice clothes to wear to work. So, I had the payroll department at work send most of my paycheck to our joint account, and a small portion to my own savings account."

Nathan pulled out her bank statement. "You have eighteen-hundred dollars in your account, and nothing has been withdrawn for three months."

"I haven't needed any new clothes since then."

Nathan left it at that, for now. "Let's talk about the affair you had." He noticed she had a fearful look on her face as she glanced at Gates. "When was this affair?"

She was hesitant to answer and looked at her attorney. "I'm ashamed it ever happened," she finally said.

"Let's begin with when it started," Nathan said.

"It started in April. Chuck's coin conventions begin then, and he leaves -- left me home alone almost every weekend. I got tired of it and started going out to some clubs."

"Who was your affair with?"

Mrs. Blanton squirmed in her seat. "I don't understand

why you need to know that."

"Who ended the affair?"

"I did. I felt guilty and broke it off."

Nathan jotted down some notes. "When was that?"

"Last month."

"Where were you the night of your husband's murder?" Nathan asked.

"I was home."

Nathan wrote something down. "Were you alone all night?"

"Yes, I was alone," she replied.

"Did Chuck find out about the affair?"

"He did," Mrs. Blanton said. "We had just had an argument about it right before the delivery of the coin where I found the invoice, which I suppose is why I was so angry and yelled at him in front of his friends."

"I'll ask again, who was your affair with?"

She took a tissue out of her pocket and dabbed her eyes.

"The affair was with me," Gates said.

"Bruce, no."

Nathan did not expect that answer. "You were the other man?"

"I was, and I don't feel good about doing that to Chuck. Besides being his attorney, I was also his friend."

"No offense, Mr Gates, but I hope I never have a friend like you," Nathan said. "I'm going to end the interview now, but I'm not done. You realize after what I've just learned you're both suspects now. Mrs. Blanton, I suggest you find a different attorney, because I'm not going further with Mr. Gates in the room with you. Mr. Gates, I would advise you do the same. Do it soon. I'll be in touch." Nathan stood and opened the door, prompting them to leave.

Hank was standing outside the room waiting for Nathan. They followed Gates and Mrs. Blanton to the corner of the hallway, and from there watched them leave the building.

"You were watching?" Nathan asked. They went to

Nathan's office.

"Only the last few minutes. How did you find out Blanton's wife had an affair?"

"I had an informant."

Hank laughed. "What informant?"

"That's not important since they admitted to the affair." Nathan sat down at his desk. "I need to talk to Blanton's two friends again. I think I'll go to Boston tomorrow to see them."

"Need me to go with you?"

"No, but I do need you for something else." He started writing on a sheet of paper. "Can you check on Bruce Gates' background? The whole works, criminal, professional, education, and financial, if you can get it. See if anything pops up." Nathan handed Hank the paper.

"No problem." Hank took the paper and left.

Nathan picked up his phone, but before he could dial, Mallory Duncan appeared at his doorway. He put the receiver back on the phone. "What can I do for you, Mallory?"

"I'm sorry to bother you. I brought you the evidence inventory list from Blanton's hotel room." She handed him the document.

"Thanks." He looked at the paper. "Did you find anything unusual?"

"Not really. There were a lot of coins, which is why it took a while to get everything logged. I recorded each coin individually."

"I don't suppose you looked up their value, did you?"

"I didn't, but I guess I could, if you really need it," she said.

"No, that's okay. I'll take care of that. Thanks, Mallory."

She left, and Nathan picked up the phone again and dialed. "Detective Denzinger, how's life in Boston today?"

The detective laughed. "Probably not as good as in Mystic. How are you, Nathan?"

"I'm pretty good. I need to interview a couple men tomorrow in Boston, and was hoping you might have a room

I could use in your building."

"I think we probably will have a room available. Do you need these interviews recorded?"

"No, nothing like that. They're not suspects at this time, just witness interviews."

"What time, and I'll reserve you a room?"

"How about the first interview at ten and the other at eleven. I can email you their names and info."

"Good. I'll get your room reserved right now," Denzinger said.

"Thanks. I appreciate it. I'd like for you to sit in on the interviews with me, if you aren't busy."

"I'm pretty sure I can squeeze that in. Anything else?"

"No, that should do it. Thanks."

"See you in the morning." Denzinger hung up.

Nathan replaced the receiver and picked up his cell phone from the desk. Turning his chair to look out the window, he dialed another number.

"Hello."

"Hi, Robin. It's Nathan Perry."

"It's nice to hear from you so soon, Nathan."

He sat back in his chair. "I'm going to be in Boston tomorrow, and was wondering if you'd like to have lunch?"

"I'd love to. What time?"

"I'm not sure. I'm interviewing some witnesses at the State Police building starting at ten o'clock. I'm hoping to be finished by noon."

"The Oyster Bar Café is about four blocks from that building. We could meet there around noon. If you think you'll be late, just give me a call. I'll do the same, if something comes up on my end."

"That sounds good. I'll see you there around noon."

"I'm looking forward to it."

Nathan ended the call, pleased that she had accepted. He checked his watch and saw it was nearly five-thirty. *Time to go home*, he thought.

He locked up all the files in his desk, grabbed his jacket, and headed out the door. As he drove by Capt's Waterfront Grill, he spotted Dana's car in the parking lot and thought he'd stop by, hoping she was dining alone. He stepped inside and found her sitting by herself at a table for two, near a window.

He approached. "Eating alone this evening?"

"I am. It's been a long day and I didn't feel like cooking dinner tonight. Would you like to join me?"

"I would." He pulled out the chair next to her and sat down. A waiter approached with a menu. "I'll have a draft beer." He looked at Dana. "Have you already ordered your food?"

"I have."

"I'll have your sirloin tips dinner," he told the waiter, who then left the table. He looked out the window at the view of the harbor at sunset. "I'll never get tired of this view."

"It is beautiful, isn't it? Does that mean that you aren't going to move back to Washington?" she asked.

"What? No, I'm not moving. Why would you asked that?"

"No special reason. How is your investigation going?" she asked, changing the subject.

Nathan was afraid this was going to be a continuation of their weekend lunch. "Dana, is everything okay between us? I mean really okay?"

She let out a deep breath. "I need to apologize for how I acted Sunday. I'm a little embarrassed to admit it, but I was jealous of you having a son."

"Why would you be jealous of that?"

"You have someone else in your life. I know we had an agreement about our relationship, but, well, I let my heart get out of control. I'm sorry."

"There's nothing to be sorry about."

The waiter interrupted their conversation when he brought Nathan's beer. "Your food should be right out," he said, before walking away.

"I spent a lot of time yesterday thinking about our

situation. I think I was right when I said that we should just be friends. I hope you understand." She took a sip of her wine.

"I understand. I agree ... friends."

They were served their food, and the conversation continued over dinner, but on a different topic.

"I actually meant to call you today. I'm working on an article about the murder. Any updates you can give me for it?" she asked, before taking a bite of food.

"Not a lot. I'm still interviewing witnesses."

"No suspects yet?"

"You know I can't tell you everything about the case." He took a drink of beer.

"So there is something." She laughed.

"Dana."

"I know. I know. Give me your official statement then."

"The official statement is that we're still investigating, and interviewing witnesses. We do have some persons of interest, but that's all they are at this time."

"Do you think the murder had anything to do with the convention? Everyone knows he was a collector," she asked.

"It's a possibility. Again, that's all I can say for now." Nathan took a bite of his food. The conversation about the murder ended there, and they enjoyed their meal together.

On Tuesday morning, Nathan arrived at Sam Denzinger's office at the Massachusetts State Police building in Boston. "Thanks for letting me use an interrogation room today," Nathan said. He took a seat in front of the desk until his witnesses showed up.

"Anytime you need it, just call," Denzinger replied. "How is your investigation going?"

"Slow, as usual." He handed him the file.

Denzinger thumbed through it. "The wife had an affair with the victim's attorney? If that doesn't scream suspect, I don't know what does." He handed the file back to Nathan.

"I kind of suspected something between them when I was interviewing them, but I didn't think it would be an affair.

He was acting as her attorney when I was questioning her, and he just admitted he was the other man. I was speechless."

"I hope they both get a better attorney."

"I agree."

Denzinger's phone buzzed and he answered it. "Thanks, Judy." He put the reciever back. "Your witnesses are here."

"Would you like to sit in with me?" Nathan asked.

"I think I would. You never know what might happen after the way your last interviews went."

Denzinger led Nathan to the room where they found Mike Metcalf and Tom Clark seated. Both officers sat across the table from them.

Nathan began. "Gentlemen, this is Detective Denzinger with the State Police. He's going to join us today. Detective, this is Mr. Metcaf and Mr. Clark."

Denzinger nodded to the men.

"Let me begin by saying you are just being interviewed as witnesses, not suspects."

"How can we be witnesses when we didn't see anything?" Metcaf asked.

Nathan could see his anxiety, but Clark looked more calm. "I understand, but you may know more than you think. That's why more questions."

"Even though you're just being interviewed as witnesses, if you would like an attorney present, you have that option," Denzinger explained.

The two men looked at each other, and then declined an attorney.

"Very well. Where were you two around three a.m. on the night Chuck was killed?" Nathan asked.

"I was in my room," Metcalf said.

"Me too," added Clark.

"Did you two share a room?"

"No, sir. We had our own rooms," Metcalf said.

"Were your rooms close to Blanton's?" Denzinger asked.

"No. Chuck was on the first floor and we were on the

second floor," Clark said.

"Were you with Blanton before you all went to your rooms?"

"We were all drinking in the bar."

"How much did you drink that night?"

"We weren't driving, so we probably drank more than we should have," Clark said.

"What about Blanton?"

"He had a lot," Clark said.

"He was getting a little loud, and the bartender finally asked him to leave," Metcalf added.

"What was he saying?" Nathan asked.

"Most of the people in the bar were collectors and he was bragging about that coin he said he had and how valuable it was," Clark said.

"A few people challenged him saying that he didn't really have it. That's when the bartender asked Chuck to leave."

"What time was that?" Denzinger asked.

"About one-thirty, I think. We left a short time later," Metcalf said.

Nathan looked through the file in front of him. "Did you ever see Bruce Gates at the Blanton's home?"

"Yes," Metcalf said. "He was there once when we were doing an inventory on Chuck's coins. Mr. Gates seemed pretty interested in the coins."

"How so?" Denzinger asked.

"He wanted to know if coins were a good investment."

"What was Chuck's answer?" Nathan asked.

"He told him that they were a great investment. He even told him about the Colonial coin.

"What was Gates' response?"

"Well, he seemed kind of impressed. He asked how much it was worth and, like everybody else, asked if he could see the coin. Chuck told him it could be priceless, and said no, he couldn't see it."

"When was that?"

Metcalf thought for a few seconds. "I think it was August."

Nathan jotted down some more notes before moving on. "Let's talk about Chuck and Sarah. How was their marriage?"

"We answered that last time," Clark said.

"Humor me, and answer again."

"They were solid."

"Well, that's not quite true," Metcalf added.

Nathan noticed the surprised look on Clark's face, then looked at Metcalf. "Would you explain?"

"Chuck confided in me that he was pretty sure Sarah was having an affair," Metcalf said.

"When did he tell you this?"

"I think it was--" A surprised look spread across Metcalf's face. "I think that was in August too. He said he came home early from a convention and Sarah wasn't home. He said it didn't look like she had been home for a couple days. When she finally got there, he said she acted pretty nervous about him getting back early."

"Did Chuck say who his wife was having an affair with?" Denzinger asked.

"He said he didn't know, but I think he suspected someone."

"Why do you think that?" Nathan asked.

"I think he started to say a name when he told me about her affair, but stopped himself, then said he didn't know who it was," Metcalf said.

"Did you suspect anyone?"

"Not really."

Nathan stood. "Gentlemen, I think that's enough today. I appreciate you coming in again. If I think of anything else, I'll call."

Metcalf and Clark stood and shook hands with Nathan and Denzinger. Clark looked at his watch. "I think we can make it to Chuck's funeral after all."

"That's today?" Nathan asked.

"Yes. In a couple hours," Clark said, before the two men left the room.

"Well, what do you think?" Denzinger asked Nathan as they walked back to Denzinger's office.

"I doubt we'll ever know for sure, but I think Chuck had an idea that Sarah's affair was with Gates."

When they reached Denzinger's office, Nathan called Chief Cabot to ask him to send either Gloria or Hank to the funeral to see how Sarah was there, and to see how comforting Gates was with her. The chief agreed, and Nathan hung up.

"Would you like to go to lunch before you head back?" Denzinger asked.

"Thanks, but I actually have a lunch date already." He called Robin Fisher to let her know he was finished.

"Hello."

"Robin, it's Nathan. I'm all finished at the police department. Can you still make it for our lunch date?"

"Yes, I can get at the restaurant in about fifteen minutes."

"Great. I'll see you there." Nathan hung up the phone and looked up at Denzinger. "Do you know Robin Fisher? She writes for the *Globe* and *Boston Magazine*?"

"I remember seeing her in Mystic after the murders. Cute lady," Denzinger said.

"My lunch date today. I'm meeting her in fifteen minutes. I better get going."

"Let me know if you need anything else with the investigation," Denzinger said.

Nathan arrived at the Oyster Bar Cafe before Robin and was seated near the front of the restaurant. He had just ordered a soda when she walked in and came over to his table. He stood and gave her a peck on the cheek. She smelled like vanilla and lavender, a scent that Katherine wore often.

"I hope you haven't been waiting long." She removed her jacket and placed it on the other chair with her purse. Nathan held her chair for her to sit. She ordered coffee to drink.

"Only a few minutes."

"Cabs were scarce, so I ended up calling for an Uber. You look good."

"So, do you. How's work been?" he asked.

"Busy, as usual. I have an appointment after lunch to interview the owner of the auction house that Blanton spoke with about selling his coin. If you'd like to tag along, you can."

"I'd like that, but are you sure the owner will talk to you, if the police are present?"

She smiled. "If he won't, you'll have to wait for me outside then."

The waiter brought their drinks and took their food order. Robin added creamer and sugar to her coffee and took a sip. "I really needed that."

"First coffee of the day?"

"I'm ashamed to say it's my fourth. I know, I know, I have a problem, but journalism is a stressful business."

"No more than police work," Nathan shot back.

" *Touché.*" She lifted her cup in a toast, and then took another sip. "So, how is your investigation going?"

Nathan laughed, remembering that Dana asked the same thing when they had dinner. "You reporters are all alike."

"What does that mean?"

"There's a reporter in Mystic that's always after me for updates on my investigations." That's all Robin needed to know about Dana.

"We all have a job to do."

"Well, since you're taking me to the auction house, I suppose I could fill you in on a few things. Blanton's wife and her attorney confirmed to me that they were having an affair. She said it ended in August. Careful when you write that up. As far as I know, the police are the only ones that know this. Although, one of Chuck's friends said that Chuck told him he suspected she was having an affair, just not who with."

"Do you think he knew it was with the lawyer?"

"I doubt we'll ever know for sure, unless Mrs. Blanton

tells me."

"Maybe if she spoke to a woman, she'd be a little forthcoming."

"That's a great idea. We have a really good female officer at the department that could talk to her."

"I actually was thinking about me," Robin said.

Nathan sat up straight. "You can't do that. If she talks to you, she might not want to talk to my officer. That could really hamper the investigation."

"I have to interview her for my article anyway. I'll give you a week for your gal to talk to her, and then I'll be calling Mrs. Blanton."

"Fair enough."

Once they finished their lunch, Nathan drove them to Alistair's Auction House. The building was not what he expected. He parked in the lot at the side of a white brick building that looked more like a warehouse than a business that auctioned off high price items.

Once inside, they were greeted in the lobby by the owner, Alistair Harris.

"Thank you for meeting with me, Mr. Harris," Robin said.

"It's my pleasure. This is actually a good day for this since Sarah isn't here," Mr. Harris said.

"Mrs. Blanton does work here. I forgot about that."

Alistair looked at Nathan.

"I'm sorry, this is Nathan Perry. He's from the Mystic Police Department, and is investigating Mr. Blanton's murder."

"I didn't realize there would be a police officer here," Alistair said.

"It was a last minute thing. He was in town and I asked him to join me. If that isn't okay, he can wait outside."

"I will have interviewed you eventually, anyway," Nathan added.

"I suppose it's fine. Come with me. We can talk in my office." Alistair led them through a door from the lobby and down a hallway to his office. "Please sit down."

Since this was Robin's interview, Nathan allowed her to take the lead with the questioning. "Do you mind if I record our interivew?" She held up her phone.

With some hesitation, Alistair agreed and she sat her phone on his desk, and hit record.

"Mr. Harris, did Mr. Blanton speak to you about selling his Colonial coin?"

"Yes, he did. Initially, he called me about it and asked if he could come and speak to me in person. I told him he could. His only condition was that I was not to say anything to his wife. Such a sad thing to happen. The funeral is today, you know. We sent flowers."

"That's nice," Robin said.

Nathan, on the other hand, wondered why Alistair was not at the funeral. He looked around the office, taking note of the paintings and statues, and wondered the value of them.

"Did he come in to talk to you?" Robin asked.

"He did, on his wife's day off."

"Did you see the coin?" Nathan asked.

"Not physically. He showed me a photo of it on his phone. He had two photos of it, the obverse and reverse."

"I'm sorry, obverse and reverse?" Nathan asked.

Alistair took a breath. "The front and back of the coin."

Nathan reminded himself to read that book about coin collecting he picked up at the library to familiarize himself with the terms.

"I told him the photos were nice, but I could not give him an appraisal of the coin unless I see it in person."

"What was his reaction to hearing that?" Robin asked.

"Well, he wasn't happy, of course. He insisted I give him an idea of the value at auction."

"Did you?" Nathan asked.

"Did I what? Oh, give him an appraisal? I told him that if the condition was as good as the photos show, it could be in the six-figure range."

"I'm sure he was happy to hear that," Robin said.

"He was, until I told him I needed possession of the coin for at least two weeks before the auction."

"When did he actually come and talk to you about selling the coin?" Nathan asked.

I think it was sometime in September, maybe during the last half of the month. I'd have to check to make sure."

"You keep records of something like that?" Nathan asked.

"It was on his wife's day off, so that would narrow it down."

"Of course. I would like that information, but there's no rush for it today," Nathan said.

"Alistair, had you met Mr. Blanton before that day?" Robin asked.

"Only when he came in here to see his wife, which wasn't often."

"Did his wife ever talk about him to you?"

"Normally, no, but a few months ago she came in sort of depressed. I asked if everything was all right, and all she said was there were problems at home."

"When was that?" Nathan asked.

"Maybe August," he replied. "It didn't last long. She was back to her old self a few days later."

"And, she never mentioned anything about her husband collecting coins?"

"She had mentioned it in passing some time ago, but I just thought it was more or less a hobby, nothing like the coin he showed me the picture of."

"Mr. Harrison, thank you for talking to us today," Robin said.

"Would it be okay to call you if I have any follow-up questions?" Nathan asked.

"Yes, that would be fine."

Nathan handed him one of his cards. "Could you call me when you figure out the date that Blanton was here to talk to you?"

"I will."

Robin and Nathan left the building, but stopped before they got into his car. "Do you think Blanton really had the coin?" Robin asked.

"The photos on his phone have me baffled. I don't remember our evidence tech saying anything about photos, but it's something I'm sure going to check out. Can I drive you back to your office?"

"No, I've already requested an Uber ride. I hope this isn't a final goodbye though." A car entered the parking lot and pulled up next to them. "That's my car."

"I promise to keep in touch." Nathan gave her a peck on the cheek.

"I'm going to hold you to that." She took one last look before getting into the car and leaving.

Chapter Five

As soon as Nathan got to work the following morning, he went straight to Mallory's office to check on Blanton's phone.

"Good morning, Nathan. What can I do for you so early?" she asked from inside the wired cage that passed for her office.

"Did you check the photos on Blanton's cell phone when you logged it in?"

"I did, along with all of the files on it. Why?"

"I interviewed someone yesterday that said Blanton showed them some photos of the coin he was wanting to sell."

Mallory started typing on her computer. "No, no photos of coins, and no emails sent with any photo attachments. However, I didn't check the memory card for any deleted photos."

"Can you do that?"

"Yes. Let me work on that and I'll get back to you."

"Thanks." Before going to his office, he checked in at the front desk, where he found Gloria sitting with handwritten papers spread out in front of her. "What in the world are you doing?" he asked.

"I'm making a presentation tonight at the Chamber of Commerce to the shop owners in Mystic about security. I'm so nervous."

"You'll do fine," he assured her. "Did you go to Blanton's funeral yesterday?"

"Yes. The chief said you needed someone to go."

"How was it? Anything to report?" Nathan sat in the chair next to her.

Gloria looked around the front lobby. Since it was early, no one was in there yet. "There weren't many people there. I saw those two men you interviewed here, and spoke to a couple of his co-workers. From what I could hear from conversations around me, I think the rest of the people there were friends or neighbors."

"What about Bruce Gates?"

"Oh, he was there, consoling Mrs. Blanton. He stayed right by her side the whole time."

"How was she doing?"

"In my opinion, faking it the whole time. She played the grieving widow to everyone, but I don't think she was grieving as much as she was trying to appear. I also went to the graveside service at the cemetery. Gates and Mrs. Blanton left together after it was over, and I followed them."

"I'm impressed, Gloria. Where did they go?"

"They went to a fancy restaurant, and were there was about an hour or so. When they left, I followed them back to her residence. It was getting late and I didn't stay, so I don't know how long Gates was there."

"You did a wonderful job. Thank you. Now, could you write that up and send it to me?"

"I already did. It should be in your inbox," she replied.

Nathan got up and patted her on the shoulder before going to his office. Then, he stopped. "I almost forgot. I may need you to interview Mrs. Blanton. Did she see you at the funeral?"

"I don't think she noticed me. She didn't make eye contact with many of the people there."

"Good. I'll let you know when."

That evening, Gloria was at the Mystic Community Center to give her presentation to the town's store owners about security and shoplifters. After she finished her presentation and the Q and A session, everyone adjourned to the refreshment table before leaving. She was happy to hear that everyone had enjoyed her talk, and they told her that they found it very informative.

Gloria noticed one gentleman stood back from the others with a drink in hand until most of the people had moved away from her. He approached and introduced himself. "Officer Wheeler, I'm James Bass. I own a pawn shop in town and need to speak to you away from these people."

They stepped out into the hallway. "Mr. Bass, what can I do for you?" she asked.

He nervously looked around. "I was wondering about that murder that happened at the coin convention. Have you figured out who done it yet?"

"We are still investigating. I'm sure you understand I can't talk about an ongoing investigation."

"There was this guy that came into my shop the day after the murder. He was acting a little odd, and kind of nervous. He was asking about rare coins, their value, and if I ever bought coins. I told him I did buy coins, but he should really go to the convention to find out more about the values. That's when he got even more nervous and said he'd already been out there the night before. Then, he just left the shop without saying anything else."

"What did this man look like?" she asked, pulling out a small notepad and pen from her pocket.

"He was about five-nine, with brown eyes. I don't know about the color of his hair because he wore one of those knit hats pulled down, kind of low like. He was dressed like he was camping, and smelled like it too."

"Mr. Bass, do you have surveillance cameras installed that would have recorded this man?"

"Yes, I do, but they run in a loop, and I don't know if its

been recorded over yet."

"Could you check tonight and see, and make a copy of it for me if the recording shows that man?"

"I can check, but I don't know how to make a copy."

Gloria thought for a few seconds. "Well then, would it be okay if I brought someone to your store tomorrow to check the tape and make a copy?"

"That would be fine." He dug a business card out of his wallet and handed it to Gloria.

She looked at the worn and slightly dirty card. "Witch City Pawn. I'm not sure what time we'll be there, but I'll try to make it sometime in the morning. Thank you for your help, Mr. Bass."

"I'll see you tomorrow, ma'am."

The next morning, Gloria, Nathan, and Mallory arrived at the pawn shop, located in a part of town that tourists didn't normally go to. Inside, they found several display cases of jewelry, knives, guns, and even a few coins. Mr. Bass came out from a back room when the door dinged upon their entry.

"Officer Wheeler, I'm glad you came," he said.

"Mr. Bass, this is Detective Perry and our IT technician, Mallory Duncan."

"It's nice to meet you, Mr. Bass," Nathan said. "Gloria tells me that you have some surveillance video we should look at."

"Yes, sir. Follow me, and I'll show you my system." Bass led them through racks of junk he obviously had obtained over many years of owning the pawn shop. Finally, they reached a room in the very rear of the building, where several monitors were on a desk, along with a VCR.

Nathan saw a lot of tapes stacked on the desk and even on the floor, within reach of the chair. He noticed a few old porn tapes, too. *Becky does Boston* was on the top of the stack.

"I came back to the store last night after I spoke with Officer Wheeler to find what you need, and to make sure it wasn't recorded over." He put a tape cartridge into the VCR and pressed play. A black and white video started playing on the TV with no sound.

They watched. "He never turns toward the camera. Are there any other cameras you have that might show his face?" Nathan asked.

"No, I only have the one camera."

"Mallory, do you think you can do some magic with the video?"

"It's an old system, and on tape, to make it worse. If I can take it back to my office, I can try and see what I can come up with," she said.

"Mr. Bass, could we have this tape? We can make a copy, and get the original back to you," Nathan said.

Bass ejected the tape. "You can have it. I have plenty of tapes to use." He handed the tape toward Nathan.

"Mallory, can I have an evidence bag to put the tape in?"

She handed Nathan a bag and he held it open for Bass to drop the tape into. "Mr. Bass, the department appreciates you coming forward with this tape. I don't suppose you know who this man is?"

"Nope. Never seen him before."

"Did you see what kind of vehicle he drove?"

"I didn't see any vehicle. He could have walked for all I know. I'm sorry I can't help anymore," Bass said.

"That's fine. What you have is good. If I have any more questions, I'll be in touch. Thank you." Nathan turned, and he and the ladies left the room, and departed the business.

They all got into his car. Before driving off, Nathan leaned over and got some anti-bacterial wipes out of the glove compartment. Handing one each to Gloria and Mallory, he kept one for himself.

"What's this for?" Gloria asked.

"Didn't you see all the porn tapes next to the desk? I bet he sits there every night watching them."

"Oh my, gosh. I think I'm going to be sick," Mallory said,

rolling down the window. "I'm going to need a lot of gloves when I work on this tape."

They all cleaned their hands with the wipes, and as soon as they returned to the department, they headed straight to the restrooms to wash their hands.

Right at quitting time, Mallory stopped by Nathan's office on her way out. She found Hank sitting in there with Nathan. "Sorry to interrupt. I wanted to fill you in on the SD card from Blanton's phone."

"Sure. Come in," he said.

Mallory sat down in the chair next to Hank. "I'm sorry I didn't catch this when I first checked the phone. The card in it is almost new. It had very little on it at all, and no photos had been deleted from it."

"So, we're looking for another card or another phone," Hank said.

"It appears so," Nathan added.

"I also went over that video from the pawn shop. I was able to enhance it a little. Here are the prints from it. I logged a set in as evidence, and also emailed you a copy too," Mallory said. "I wish I could have done more with them."

Nathan looked at the photos she brought. "These are better, but you still can't see his face well enough for an ID." He handed the photos to Hank.

"But, if this is the guy and we find him, we could probably match him to this," Hank said.

"Mallory, you did the best you could and I really appreciate it. Thanks."

"You're welcome. See you tomorrow."

"Did you make it through the tape without getting sick?" Nathan asked, chuckling.

"I hope I never have to process any evidence like that again." She left.

"What was that all about?" Hank asked.

"There was a stack of porn tapes next to the desk where the pawn shop guy had his recording equipment. When I told

Mallory about the tapes, once we got into my car, I thought I was going to have to clean up vomit."

He laughed, along with Nathan. "What's next with the case?" Hank asked.

Nathan let out a deep breath. "Would you mind taking these photos out to the Mystic Inn and showing them around, especially in the bar, and see if anyone knows this guy, or if he was seen out there the night of the murder?"

"I can do that tomorrow," Hank said.

Hank got up and left. Nathan started getting ready to go home too, when his desk phone rang. "Perry."

"Hello, detective. I'm glad I caught you before you left for the day."

"Robin, it's nice to hear from you." He sat back down. "To what do I owe the pleasure?"

"I learned some information that I thought you'd be interested in."

"About the Blanton murder?"

"Yes. A source told me that Blanton had a half a million-dollar life insurance policy with Mrs. Blanton as the beneficiary."

"That is interesting." He took the Blanton file out of his desk drawer and started making notes. "Who gave you this information?"

"You know I can't reveal my source."

"Let me ask you this, then, how reliable is this source of yours?"

"Pretty reliable. They gave me all the life insurance information right down to the policy number."

"Are you going to share that information with me, or do I have to bribe you for it?" he asked.

"I'm sure I could be persuaded to share, for the right price."

Nathan leaned back in his chair and smiled. "How about a weekend in an oceanside home with a roaring fireplace, lobster with wine, and good company?"

"That sounds like a perfect weekend. I can drive down right after work tomorrow."

"Outstanding. I'll get the food I need on the way home tonight. Anything special you want?"

"Let me bring the wine."

"And, don't forget the life insurance information."

Robin laughed. "That's all you want me for, isn't it?"

"Oh, I can think of a few other things you're good for."

"I'll see you tomorrow."

"Bye." Nathan hung up the phone and left for the day.

Midmorning on Friday, Nathan called Sarah Blanton. "Mrs. Blanton, this is Detective Perry from the Mystic Police Department. How are you today?"

"I'm fine, Detective. What can I do for you?"

"I was wondering if you could come to the police department Monday morning? I have a few more questions for you."

"In Mystic?"

"Yes."

He heard her let out a deep breath. "Can't you just ask me over the phone?"

"Actually, no. This is a murder investigation; everything needs to be in person."

"I know it's an investigation. How much longer is this going to go on? The life insurance company from Chuck's work won't pay out until I'm cleared as a suspect, so his funeral has not been paid for yet."

"I understand, ma'am. If you can just come in, this could bring us closer to clearing you," Nathan said.

"Alright, what time should I be there?"

"Could you be here by ten a.m.?"

"I'll be there." She hung up her phone.

Nathan had rattled her. Good, that's what he wanted. He then called Gloria and asked her to come back to his office.

A few minutes later, Gloria stuck her head in his door. "I'll be in as soon as I get some coffee."

He thought that sounded like a good idea and grabbed his cup and followed her into the breakroom. "Let me pour that for you." He filled her cup, and while she added creamer to her coffee, he filled his. They walked back to his office.

"Sarah Blanton will be in Monday morning at ten and I want you to interview her. I think she might feel a little more like talking if a female does the interrogation."

"I'll do what I can, but I don't really know what to ask her," Gloria responded.

"That's why I called you back here. I want to go over everything with you. First, she thinks I'm going to talk to her, but I want you to tell her I'm not here, so you're going to talk to her instead. I'm going to stay out of sight, but I'll be in the viewing room, watching."

"What if I forget to ask something important?"

"You won't, but we call always ask her later." He handed a file folder to her. "I made you a copy of what you need to know for the interview, including a list of questions. Don't be afraid to go off script. Mainly, we need to know about the half-a-million-dollar insurance policy, and a little more about her affair with Gates."

Gloria looked through the file. "What half-a-million-dollar insurance policy? I don't see anything in here about that."

"I don't have all of the information about the policy yet, but I'll have it by Monday morning. All I know right now is that Blanton had a life insurance policy on him for that amount. Allegedly, his wife is the beneficiary, but again, I'll know more about it by Monday. Look over the file. Don't be afraid to make notes. This file is yours. If you have any questions, I'll be back here after lunch. Take it home with you and study it over the weekend, if you want."

Gloria took a deep breath. "Thank you for your confidence in me. I'll do the best I can." She got up to leave.

"I know you will."

Nathan took a drink of his coffee, and then picked up his

phone to call Hank.

"Hi, Nathan. What do you need?"

"Good morning. Are you busy today?"

"Not too busy. What's up?"

"How about meeting me for lunch at the Witch's Brew in a few minutes?" Nathan asked.

"Sure. I just finished showing that picture around at the Mystic Inn. I can fill you in on what I found."

"I'll see you there." He hung up the phone, grabbed his jacket, and left.

Since Hank was across town, Nathan arrived first and took a seat at a booth near the back of the establishment near the counter. He waved at Ginger as he sat down.

"Coffee?" she asked from the counter.

"Just a Coke today." He looked at the people in the restaurant. It was busy today.

"Here you go." Ginger sat his drink on the table and handed him a menu.

"Hank will be joining me in a few minutes."

She sat down across the table from him. "What's going on today, Detective?"

"Same as always," he replied. "You're busy today."

"It's October, the leaves are changing, and Halloween is around the corner. The tourists have arrived," she said, spreading her arms out.

"That's good for business, right?"

"It is, but the talk of the day is still that murder. You gonna solve that soon?"

"I sure hope so." He wanted to change the subject. "Hey, you wouldn't have a big pot I could borrow for the weekend, would you?" He took a drink of his Coke.

"Maybe. What do you need it for?"

"I'm having a weekend guest and I wanted to boil some lobster."

"Gotcha. Dana coming over?"

He hesitated. "No, someone else."

"Oh, I see. You've got your hooks into a new girl," she said.

"Something like that."

"Yeah, I got a pot you can use. I'll drop it off at your place on the way home tonight."

"Just leave it by the front door. No need to come in."

The door dinged and Hank walked into the café. Ginger laughed as she got up. "You got it, stud." She looked at Hank. "Coke for you too?"

"No, I think I'll have coffee today. It's kind of cold out," he said.

Ginger went for his coffee as Hank sat down.

"You want to look at the menu?" Nathan asked.

"Nah, I know what's on it."

Ginger brought Hank his coffee and sat it on the table. "What do you guys want to eat today?"

"I'll take your special," Nathan said.

"Me too," Hank added.

Nathan handed Ginger the menu and she headed to the kitchen.

"What did you find out at the hotel?" Nathan asked.

Hank took a sip of coffee before answering. "None of the hotel staff recognized the guy in the photo, but when I went to the bar, the bartender and a waitress knew him."

"That's good."

"Not exactly. They didn't know his name, but did say he was in the bar the night that Blanton was killed. They said he was kind of quiet and just seemed to be listening to what the coin people were talking about."

"Was he drinking?"

"Yes, but he paid cash."

"Did they know long he stayed?" Nathan asked.

"Not really. He sat alone, paid for each drink when he got it, instead of running a tab, and then he was just gone. No knew when he left."

"That's too bad, but at least we have him at the scene."

Ginger came back with their lunch plates. "Here you go. Can I get you anything else?"

"Nothing for me."

"I'm good too."

Before Ginger could walk away from the table, the door dinged again. "Well, looky there."

Nathan looked up and saw Dana Tyler walk in with a gentleman. She saw him and started walking toward them with her friend following.

"Hello, officers, Ginger," Dana said. "I'd like for you to meet Joseph Royce. He's a professor over at Salem State College. Joe, this is Ginger. She owns the place, and this is Detective Nathan Perry and Officer Hank McCoy."

"It's nice to meet you all," Royce said.

Ginger was smiling from ear to ear. "It's good to meet you too. What can I bring you two to drink?"

"Sweet tea for me," Dana said.

"Coffee is fine," Royce replied. Ginger stepped away.

"How is the investigation going, Nathan?" Dana asked.

"Slow." He took a bite of his lunch.

"Well, you make sure and keep me informed for the newspaper."

"I will."

She stepped away, with Royce following her like a little puppy. They took a booth across the room.

Nathan stared at the new couple as Royce sat with his back to the room and Dana faced toward him.

"You okay?" Hank asked.

"What? Oh, yes, I'm fine." He turned his attention back to Hank. "I was thinking that we need to have Alex Gold from the convention take a look at the photo. Maybe she will recognize him."

"It's worth a shot."

"I'll give her a call when I get back to the office," Nathan said.

They finished their lunch and Hank went back on patrol.

Nathan took his time before leaving. Finally, he got up and walked toward the front door, passing Dana and her friend. "Have a nice day," he said to them as he passed.

Back at his office, he dialed Alex Gold's number. "Miss Gold, Nathan Perry calling from the Mystic Police Department."

"Hello, Detective. What can I do for you?"

"We have a photo of a possible suspect. I was hoping you could come to Mystic and take a look at it. He was seen around the hotel, but we haven't identified him."

"It's just a photo, not a line up, or anything like that?" she asked.

Nathan held back a chuckle. "I just need for you to look at a photo."

"Can't you email it to me to look at, so I don't have to drive all the way to Mystic? It seems like that would be so much easier and faster."

"I wish I could, but I can't release the photo to anyone. I really need for you to come today, if at all possible."

"Very well. I can be there in a couple hours."

"Thank you. I do appreciate it. I'll see you then." Nathan hung up the phone.

Late in the afternoon, Alex Gold showed up at the police department. The male officers stopped and stared as Nathan led her down the hallway to his office. She wore a tight-fitting red dress, blonde hair cascading down her shoulders, and four-inch heels.

"Please have a seat," he said, closing the door. "I really appreciate you coming today."

"Can we get this over with. I have plans for this evening."

"Of course. He took the photo out from a file on his desk and handed it to her. "Do you recognize this man?"

She stared at the photo for several seconds and then handed it back to Nathan. "He was at the convention early in the week and asked me for a job."

"Did you hire him?"

"Are you kidding? Look at him. He was dirty and smelled

of stale cigarettes and alcohol."

"Did he fill out an application or give you his name and address?"

"I think he said his name was William Giles. That's all I know; no application, and I have no idea what his address is. I didn't have a job for him, so I sent him on his way."

Nathan made some notes in the file. "Did you see him anymore that week at the convention?"

"No. Did he kill Chuck Blanton?" she asked.

"We're not sure. At this point, he's only a person of interest. Do you know anything else about Mr. Giles?"

"You know what I know. Was Blanton's coin ever found?"

"Not yet."

"If it's discovered, will it go to his wife?"

Nathan thought that was an odd question. "If it's found, and once the case is solved, it will likely go to Mrs. Blanton. Why?"

"I'd still like to auction it off at one of my shows. Do you have any idea what the commission would be on a valuable coin like that?"

Now, it made sense. It was all about money. "I'm sure it would be a lot. You'd have to speak to Mrs. Blanton about auctioning it off, if it's found. Thank you for coming in. I think that's all I need for now."

Miss Gold stood and pressed down the wrinkles of her dress as much as she could. "Next time, you'll have to come to me. I'm not driving back here again." She marched out of the office, hips swaying with every step.

Nathan turned his attention back to the case. He pulled up the Massachusetts BMV database and entered William Giles. Instantly, the information popped up on the screen. Giles was twenty-seven years old, brown hair, brown eyes, five-nine, and one hundred-seventy pounds. His last known residence was listed as homeless, Boston, Massachusetts.

At least there was a photo, much better than the one from the pawn shop. He put out a BOLO on William Giles to all the police departments in the region. Lastly, he emailed the information specifically to Sargent Donnelly for the morning briefings, to his Boston Police Department contact, and to Sam Denzinger at the State Police. With his tasks finished for the day, he was ready to head home for a relaxing weekend with Robin Fisher.

He arrived home and quickly showered and shaved to get ready for his evening. Robin arrived soon afterward. Nathan opened the front door for her and took her overnight bag. They walked into the living room.

"I have wine," she said, holding up a bag.

"You can put that in the refrigerator, and I'll take your bag to the bedroom." He placed her bag on the bed and then turned around to find she had quickly put the wine away and followed him into his room. "Well, hello."

She put her arms around him and stretched up to give him a kiss. "I couldn't wait to do that," she said.

He smiled. "Do you want to finish what you just started, or do you want to go out to dinner?" he asked.

"Do you have anything here for dinner?"

"Just the lobster I got for tomorrow."

"We better go out to dinner and continue this when we get back." She took a step back. "I probably should freshen up a little before we go."

"The bathroom is in there." He motioned toward a door. "I'll wait for you in the living room."

Once she was ready, Nathan took her to Capt's Waterfront Grill for dinner, and they were seated at his favorite table overlooking the harbor.

"It's beautiful here." The lights from the few ships still in the harbor for autumn were bright and colorful. "This has to be one of the most visually stunning views in the Northeast."

"I love the harbor at night. It's definitely a high point of living here." They were served their drinks. "Let's get business out of the way first. Tell me about Blanton's life insurance policy."

She took a paper out of her purse and pushed it over in front of him. "Here's what I dug up."

He read over the document that showed all the information about the policy, number, face value, cash value, and most importantly, Sarah Blanton as beneficiary. "You don't have who took the policy out."

"It's the only missing information. I was hoping you'd be able to get that from Mrs. Blanton."

"She's coming in on Monday to talk to us again. I'll see if we can get that from her. Can I keep this?" he asked, referring to the paper.

"That's why I brought it."

Nathan folded the paper and placed it in his shirt pocket. He decided not to tell Robin about William Giles just yet. He doubted she was sharing everything she knew, and he felt the same way.

At the end of the evening, Nathan paid their bill and they got up to leave. At the door, they ran into Dana Tyler and Joseph Royce coming into the restaurant. Dana's eyes widened when she saw Nathan with Robin. He did his best to hide his reaction to seeing her and Royce together again. "Hello, Dana. Mr. Royce."

"Good evening, Nathan." Dana looked at Robin.

"Oh, this is Robin Fisher. Robin, this is Dana Tyler from the Mystic News."

"I know Miss Fisher," Dana said. She looked at Robin. "I've read many of your stories."

"Thank you," Robin replied. "I'm afraid I haven't read your newspaper, but I'm sure you do a good job. The paper has an excellent reputation."

Nathan could see this could erupt into something that didn't need to happen in public. "I think we should probably get going. Enjoy your evening." He took Robin's elbow and led her out of the restaurant and to his truck. He pulled out onto the street and headed toward home.

"Well, that was an interesting encounter. Do you want to

share what it was all about?" Robin asked.

"That? That wasn't anything, but I thought you two were going to start exchanging punches."

"You know what I'm talking about. There's clearly something between you two. Are you going to tell me what it is, or do I need to call Miss Tyler on Monday to find out?"

"There's really nothing to tell. Dana and I dated in high school."

Robin laughed. "You're talking to an investigative reporter, remember? Come on, spill it."

Nathan felt things closing in on him. Now, he knew how some of his suspects must feel when he questioned them. "We may have gone out a few times since I returned to Mystic, but she and I agreed that we didn't want a relationship with each other. Besides, she's out with that professor guy tonight."

Robin laughed again. "You seriously didn't agree on a friends with benefits deal with her, did you?"

"Stop laughing. It's not funny. It doesn't matter anymore, because she ended our relationship when I became a father."

"She ended it because of that?" Robin said.

"I think so. She's not been the same friendly person since I got back from his birth."

"She's not worth it then."

Nathan turned the truck onto his driveway. "Can we stop talking about this. It's just plain weird and making me very uncomfortable." He parked the truck and turned the engine off.

"You're right. This isn't a topic that we should be discussing." She moved over next to him and turned his head toward her, giving him a kiss. "I think it's time to go inside."

When they stepped onto the porch, they found a large metal pot sitting by the door. "What's this?" Robin asked.

"I needed a pot to boil the lobster in and borrowed one from my housekeeper. She said she'd drop it off."

Robin picked up the pot and removed the lid. "There's a note inside."

Nathan took the note and read it to himself and laughed. "What does it say?"

"You wouldn't get the joke." He took her inside and closed the door behind them.

Chapter Six

Saturday afternoon was a beautiful day with sunny skies and cool temperatures. Nathan had set up a propane cooker on his deck to use to boil the lobsters. Inside, Robin was preparing the side dishes.

Nathan came in the house to get more water to fill the pot on the cooker. "What are you fixing?"

"I brought the ingredients for cole slaw and pasta salad."

"Two of my favorites. Did you see the apple crisp I got for dessert?"

"Yes, it looked really good, but not your usual supermarket pie."

"It's not. My housekeeper owns a little restaurant in town and I bought one of her made-from-scratch desserts. It's the best in town. I have ice cream to go with it too."

He took the last of the water out to the pot and lit the flame. After Robin finished the side dishes, she joined him. "I brought you a cup of cocoa."

He took the cup from her. "Thanks. That's perfect for this weather." Steam rose from the pot of water, but it wasn't boiling yet. "I've been thinking about that life insurance policy. How could someone take a policy out like that without Blanton knowing about it? Wouldn't he have to sign something and take a physical exam? That's a big policy to not at least have medical information."

"I suppose that's true, unless you could find a crooked insurance agent. Once Blanton was dead, other than the purchaser and agent, who would know Blanton didn't know anything about it."

"Exactly, and they could have forged his signature," Nathan said. With the water now boiling, he dropped two lobsters into the pot and placed the lid on top. "The information you gave me about the insurance only had the policy number, not the company name. Your source didn't have that?"

She took a sip of her cocoa. "No, just the policy number. I'm going to go set the table." She quickly went into the house.

Again, Nathan believed she was holding back some information about that policy. He didn't really blame her. Like him, she had a job to do, but they had agreed to share information. He wouldn't push her on it. After all, he wasn't telling her everything either.

A few minutes later, he brought the lobsters in and they enjoyed a wonderful dinner. That evening, Nathan lit a fire in the fireplace, and they spent the evening getting to know each other even more.

Monday morning started off with him being late to work. Robin had left Sunday afternoon, and he spent the rest of the day and evening watching football. When he got to work, he needed coffee. He picked up the cup from his desk and immediately saw the moldy mess inside. He had forgotten to wash it before he left Friday. In the breakroom, he greeted the other officers, washed his cup, filled it, and headed back to his office.

"It's about time you got in," Gloria said, standing by his door. "Where have you been?" She followed him into his office.

"I stayed up late watching the Patriots game last night and forgot to set my alarm when I went to bed. I overslept." He sat down at his desk and took a drink of coffee. "Here's the information about the life insurance policy you'll need when you interview Mrs. Blanton today." He pushed a sheet of paper across the desk toward her.

Gloria picked up the paper and looked over it. "There's no company name. What company is the policy with?"

"That's the only information I don't have. Hopefully, you can get that with your questioning."

"What if she brings an attorney?"

"I'm hoping she's been too busy with the funeral to get a new attorney yet, but if she does, you can handle it."

"I hope so. A good attorney won't let her answer any of my questions."

"A good attorney wouldn't even let her come here, and since we haven't heard from her, I'm counting on her coming alone." He took another drink from his cup. "I have confidence in you, Gloria. You'll do fine. Let me know when she gets here. Take her to Interrogation Room Two, then give me enough time to get into the viewing room before you bring her back."

"I'll buzz you when she gets here." Gloria got up and left.

At five minutes after ten, Gloria called to say that Sarah Blanton had arrived. "I'm going to the viewing room right now," Nathan replied. He got up, turned his office light off, closed the door, and went to the viewing room.

A few minutes later, Gloria brought Mrs. Blanton into the room. Nathan was glad to see she was alone, no attorney with her. The two ladies sat down. Gloria opened the file up in front of her.

"Mrs. Blanton, as I told you, Detective Perry was unexpectedly called away and he asked me to fill in for him."

"I understand. I'm glad I didn't have to reschedule this, Officer Wheeler."

"Please, call me Gloria. May I call you Sarah? I think that helps put us both at ease. I don't do a lot of questioning."

"Yes, you can."

"Sarah, I do need to remind you that you were read your rights when you were last questioned. Do you remember those rights?"

"Yes."

"I see you don't have an attorney present today. Do you wish have one with you?"

"No. Let's get this over with."

"When you were questioned last time, you and Mr. Gates admitted to having an affair. How did that affair start?"

"Bruce was Chuck's attorney. He stopped by one weekend when Chuck was at a convention. I was lonely, and since Chuck wasn't there, I asked Bruce in for coffee. After that, he started coming by more often, and things just sort of happened."

"What made you end it?" Gloria asked.

"When it started, I felt Chuck was paying more attention to his coins than to me. Then, he took me away for a weekend in Maine. After that, things became better between us. After a while, I started feeling guilty about the affair and decided to end it."

"Do you know if Chuck ever found out about the affair?"

"I really don't know. I hope he didn't."

"How did Mr. Gates feel about the affair ending? Would he have said anything to Chuck?" Gloria asked.

"When I told Bruce it was over, he said he understood. He didn't seem upset or anything like that. After Chuck's death, I asked Bruce if he ever told him about the affair and he said no."

"Do you believe him?"

"Yes, I do."

Gloria jotted down something in the file. "Do you know if Chuck had more than one cell phone?"

"More than one? He had a phone and I have a phone. He might have had a work phone, but I don't remember him ever bringing one home. Oh, I almost forgot. I think I found the coin he wanted to sell."

Sarah bent over to get something out of her purse. Gloria turned around and looked at the mirrored wall behind her, hoping Nathan could read her thoughts.

"Here it is." She handed Gloria a small box.

Gloria took the box, stood, and walked over to the mirror when she opened the box so Nathan could see it too. She turned back to Sarah. "Where did you find the coin?"

"I was going through some of Chuck's clothes, you know, to donate to the church, and I found it in a pair of pants. Lucky, eh?"

"Yes, lucky. You realize we'll have to take this into evidence?"

"But, it's mine now. I want to sell it."

"I understand, but it's now evidence in your husband's murder investigation. If you don't turn it over, we'll get a warrant for it. It will be returned to you at the conclusion. We'll issue you a receipt for it. That will guarantee its return."

"Well, if you promise."

"I do. I only have a few more questions. I understand that Chuck had a rather large life insurance policy."

"He had a ten-thousand-dollar policy from work and that will just barely pay for his funeral expenses," she said.

Gloria wrote that down. "No, I'm talking about a larger policy, five-hundred-thousand dollars."

Sarah started chewing on her nails. "Where did you hear that from?"

"It's all part of our investigation. Would you tell me about that policy?"

She hesitated for several seconds before answering. "Chuck took the policy out on himself. It's through Boston Life," she finally said.

"Those premiums must have been quite expensive. How did he pay them?" Gloria asked.

"He, ahm, he borrowed the money from a friend. He didn't tell me who."

"You're the beneficiary of that policy. Has anyone come forward asking you for the repayment of that loan?"

"No, no one. Are we finished here? I really need to get back home."

"One more question, when did Chuck take the policy out?"

"I think it was about a year ago."

Gloria was out of questions. "I think we're finished. If you'll come with me, we'll get this coin logged in as evidence, and get you that receipt. Has anyone touched this besides you since you found it?"

"No, just me."

"Fine. Please, come with me." Gloria took her to see Mallory, who issued her a receipt for the coin.

After Mrs. Blanton left, Gloria went back to Nathan's office where they went over the information that she had discovered from the questioning.

"You did a wonderful job, Gloria," Nathan said. "I'm very proud of you."

"We need to go look at that coin." They both got up and went to see Mallory.

When they got to her cage, they could see she was working on something. "Mallory, can we disturb you for a few minutes?" Nathan asked.

"Sure. What do you need?"

"I'd like to see the coin that Sarah Blanton brought in."

"That's what I'm working on now. I just dusted it for fingerprints."

"Were there any?" he asked.

"Just smudges on something that small. I really didn't think I'd get anything, but wanted to try anyway." She brought the coin over for him to see.

"It looks old enough, but I don't know if it's the coin he wanted to sell or not. I'm going to have to have an expert look at it." Nathan decided to go to lunch and gave the coin back to Mallory, to return it to the evidence box.

The lunch crowd had already cleared out of the Witch's Brew Café when he arrived to eat. He sat at his usual booth near the counter, and Ginger brought him a menu. "How did your weekend go?" she asked.

"It was very nice. Thanks for the use of the cooking pot and your apple crisp was delicious." He looked at the menu.

"It's one of my best sellers. What will you have today?"

"I liked a bowl of clam chowder and a Coke."

The door dinged and Ginger looked up to see who came in. "Don't look now, but your old girlfriend just came in."

Nathan did look and saw Dana. He waved to her to join him. "It's okay," he told Ginger.

"Good afternoon, Miss Dana. What I can bring you today?" Ginger asked.

"Your special is chowder today, right?" She removed her coat and sat down across from Nathan.

"Yes ma'am, it is."

"I'll take that and some coffee.

"Coming right up." Ginger turned and left.

"How's the investigation going?" Dana asked Nathan.

"We have a few persons of interest, but no specific suspects yet."

"Is that on the record?"

"Yes, you can print that."

"Thanks."

Nathan sensed Dana's coolness toward him. She was all business. "We questioned Blanton's wife again this morning. She brought a coin in that she thinks might be the one that he was trying to sell."

"That's something new."

"It is, but we don't know for sure if it's really the coin. I guess I'm going to have to take it to Boston to have someone evaluate it. That's going to cost some money, and neither the chief or the mayor is going to like that expense, and that's off the record."

Dana smiled at his little joke. Maybe he had broken through that icy shell.

Ginger brought their food. "Can I get you anything else?" she asked. Both indicated no, so she went to check on the few other customers in the café.

"Why don't you ask Paul Hobbs to authenticate it?" Dana suggested. She took a sip of the hot chowder.

"Who?"

"Haven't you read any of my articles in the paper about the murder?"

"I'm sorry, but I haven't picked up the paper for the last week. I've just been too busy. Who is this guy?"

"Paul Hobbs is a local coin enthusiast that I interviewed for my articles. I'm sure he would check your coin without charging you. He's been a collector since he was a kid."

"That would be great. Not only would it save the department some money, but it would save me a trip to Boston. How do I find him?"

"When I get back to my office, I'll call you with his contact information," Dana said.

They both concentrated on their chowder, but the silence became almost uncomfortable.

Eventually, Nathan spoke up. "How's your professor guy?"

"My professor guy?"

"Yeah, you know, Joe. Tell me about Joe, like how you met."

"He teaches English and Journalism at the State College in Salem. We met when the newspaper sent me over to talk to one of his classes."

"You two must have hit right off," Nathan said.

"It's nothing serious."

"Like our relationship was nothing serious," he snapped back.

Dana stopped eating and just looked at Nathan. Finally, she placed her spoon on the table and got up. She took her coat and went to the counter to pay her bill.

"Seriously, you're going to leave?" he said.

She didn't answer, but marched out of the café without looking back at him. He dropped his spoon into the bowl and looked over at Ginger, who just shrugged her shoulders. He knew he shouldn't have said it, but it came out before he could stop. He felt like an idiot.

He returned to the police department after lunch, and soon thereafter, Gloria buzzed him.

"There's a call for you on line three from the newspaper."

"Thanks." Thinking it was Dana, he picked up the receiver and answered with an apology. "I'm sorry about earlier."

"Excuse me?" the caller said.

"Is this Dana Tyler?" he asked.

"No, this is Cindy Davis. I work with Miss Tyler."

"Oh, I thought it was Dana calling me. What can I do for you, Cindy?" There was that idiot feeling again.

"Miss Tyler wanted me to call you with the contact information of Paul Hobbs."

Nathan wrote down the information. "Thank you, Cindy. Please tell Miss Tyler that I apologize for my comments over lunch."

Before Nathan called Hobbs, he went to the breakroom and looked through the recycle bin to find the papers with Dana's articles about the murder. He found a few issues and took them back to his office to read through.

The article about Hobbs said he had collected coins since he was a child, but he didn't get serious about it until adulthood. He was also a member of several numismatics organizations and a recognized expert in the field. After finishing the articles, he called Hobbs to schedule a meeting with him for the following day.

Before Nathan left on Tuesday to see Hobbs, he went to Mallory's office to sign out the coin. "I'm going to need that coin from yesterday for a few hours today," he said.

Mallory retrieved the coin from the vault and had Nathan sign the log sheet. He took the coin, housed in a small plastic bag, and slipped it into his pocket.

He followed the directions from his GPS device and arrived at Hobbs' home just outside of the Mystic city limits around one-o'clock. Nathan knocked, and a middle-aged man opened the door. "Mr. Hobbs?"

"Yes. You must be Detective Perry," the man said. "Please come in." Hobbs took him to his home office that looked a lot like the room that Blanton had in his home for his collection, with one exception. In addition to the lighted magnifier attached to his desk, he also had an overhead projector that showed an image of a coin on the wall.

"How much do you know about numismatics?" Hobbs asked.

"Well, I only learned what that word meant a few days ago, if that tells you anything."

"That's okay. I didn't know what it meant when I started out too."

"Where you at the convention here in Mystic?"

"I was out there for a short time on Friday. I don't usually deal with collectors that I don't know. I limit myself to known collectors or auction houses. There is less chance of buying a fake that way. Please sit down." Hobbs brought a chair over for Nathan and they both sat.

"Had you ever met Chuck Blanton?" Nathan asked.

"No, I didn't know him, but I understand from Miss Tyler that he had a rare coin to sell."

"That's our understanding. His wife found a coin that she thinks is the one he wanted to sell and brought it to the police department yesterday." Nathan took the coin out of his pocket and handed it to Hobbs. "The collectors I've talked to said he wanted to sell a Brasher Doubloon."

Hobbs looked at the coin, turning it over to look at both sides and also the edges. "This isn't a Brasher Doubloon."

"It's not?"

Hobbs retrieved a book from his shelf and thumbed through it, and stopped on a page, showing it to Nathan. "This is what a Brasher Doubloon looks like."

Nathan looked at the book and then at the coin. It was not the coin he thought it was. "So, it's a fake?"

"Not a fake. It's a real coin, just not the one you thought

it was. What you have here is a Massachusetts Authorized Issue half-cent coin, minted in 1787."

"Is it worth anything?' Nathan asked.

"If it were an uncirculated coin, it could be worth around four-thousand dollars. This coin isn't in very good condition. If it were in better shape, you would be able to read Massachusetts on the front of it. In its current condition, it's probably worth no more than a hundred twenty-five dollars."

"How much do you think a Brasher Doubloon could bring in an auction?"

"It's hard to say. If the right collectors were bidding on it, it could go as high as three million," Hobbs said.

"Definitely worth killing for."

"If you say so." Hobbs laughed.

"How many of them are still around?"

"There were fifty minted, but only four are known to be in collections."

"Mr. Hobbs, thank you so much for your help. You have educated me on numismatics, if only a little."

"My pleasure. Call on me anytime you need more information." He and Nathan shook hands and Hobbs showed him to the door.

"I may just do that."

Nathan returned to the police department and went to the evidence locker to return the coin. He found Gloria there, talking to Mallory. "Good afternoon, ladies."

"Is that the coin?" Gloria asked.

"According to our expert, it's not the coin."

"I'm disappointed," Mallory said.

"He said this coin is only worth around a hundred dollars." He handed Mallory the coin, and she had him sign the log sheet showing when it was returned. She immediately took it back to the vault.

"What do we do now?" Gloria asked.

"I don't know. I'm at a total loss. I think I'm just going to go home, and try not to think about it until tomorrow,"

Nathan said.

Hank was waiting for Nathan when he got to his office the next morning. "Good morning."

Nathan walked into his office and sat his travel cup on his desk, hanging his coat on the wall hook. "I hope it's a good morning," he said. "Do you have something?"

"Maybe. I've been doing that background check on Bruce Gates you asked me to do."

Nathan sat down. "Find anything interesting?"

"Maybe. He graduated from Boston College Law School and then went to work for a mid-size law firm. He worked there for about three years before he left to start his own practice. He took two clients with him from the old firm. That got him established. He was doing pretty good and even hired a couple lawyers to handle some cases."

Nathan took a drink of his coffee. "What kind of law did he practice?"

"Mostly, corporate law, but all of his clients were small business, rather than corporations. He went into debt pretty bad when he moved to a larger office. Then, he lost some clients."

"Why did the clients leave?" Nathan asked.

"One of his attorneys left, and a few clients went with that attorney. The firm's income was greatly reduced."

"When this happen?"

Hank looked at the notes in his notebook. "August. Wasn't that when one of Blanton's friends said Gates became interested in his coins?"

"Yes, it was. What about Gates bank account? Were you able to get any information on that?"

"The judge said I didn't have enough evidence on Gates to get a warrant for that."

"When Sarah Blanton came in yesterday, Gloria questioned her about a large life insurance policy for half-a-million dollars on her husband. She said the policy was with Boston Life Insurance Company and that Chuck took the policy out, but I don't buy it. Do you think the judge will give us a warrant to find out who that policy was sold to?"

"All we can do is request it," Hank said.

"I'll do the paperwork for that this afternoon, but I need to make some phone calls first."

Hank got up to leave, then Nathan remembered something. "Oh, Mrs. Blanton also brought in a coin yesterday that she said was the one that her husband was wanting to sell. I checked with an expert. It wasn't the coin."

"I wonder if she knew that or really thought it was the coin."

"That's a good question. I'm going to call her today to tell her and see what her reaction is," Nathan said.

Hank left for his patrol and Nathan started on the paperwork for the warrant for the life insurance. Around eleven-o'clock, he decided to call Sarah Blanton.

"Hello," a male voice answered over the phone.

"Is this the Blanton residence?" Nathan asked.

"Yes, it is."

"Can I speak to Sarah Blanton? This is Detective Perry from the Mystic Police Department." The next thing Nathan heard was Sarah Blanton's voice.

"Detective, hello. What can I do for you?"

"Was that Bruce Gates that answered the phone," Nathan asked.

"Yes. He's handling Chuck's estate."

Nathan actually wasn't surprised to hear that Gates was still in Mrs. Blanton's life. It made him wonder even more about Gates as a suspect. "I thought you'd like to know that I had that coin you found evaluated, and it is not the coin that Chuck wanted to sell at the convention."

"That wasn't the coin? I don't know what to say. I was hoping it was."

"The expert that looked at the coin said it was valued at one-hundred twenty-five dollars. Since it isn't the coin in question, we don't need it as evidence. You can come to pick it up whenever you want."

"I have to come to Mystic again? Hold on a minute."

Nathan could hear mumbling, and he knew she was talking to Gates.

"Detective, couldn't you mail the coin to me?" she asked.

"I'm afraid not. We will need for you to sign it out of evidence."

"Well, I'm not sure when I can drive down there."

"No matter when, it will be with the evidence technician when you come."

"All right. Thank you." Mrs. Blanton ended the call.

Nathan hung up his phone, shaking his head.

Over lunch, Nathan took the paperwork for the warrant to get bank information on Bruce Gates to Judge Mason to sign. He had to leave the document with the secretary, since the judge was out for the rest of the day.

When he returned to the police department, he started calling some of the homeless shelters in Boston to inquire about William Giles. He found over fifty shelters listed in his internet search. Many of them only housed women, so he could rule those out.

After calling the first ten in the list, he kept getting the same answer; due to confidentiality, they could not confirm that Giles was living there, but they could take a message to pass along if the person showed up. In every case, Nathan did not leave a message.

He dialed the next number.

"Harrison Street Shelter, how can I help you?"

"I'm trying to locate a man named William Giles. It's very important that I contact him," Nathan said.

"I'm sorry, sir. I really can't tell you if he is here or not. I'm not allowed to release that type of information."

"I'm Detective Nathan Perry from the Mystic Police Department and Mr. Giles may be a witness in a murder investigation. It's very important for me to find him."

The lady on the other end of the call paused before

answering. "All I will say is that most of the men that stay here come into the building around six o'clock when we start serving dinner. If you were here around that time, you might just find the person you're looking for."

"Six o'clock. Thank you very much." He hung up the phone. It was the best lead he'd had so far. Now, he needed to make sure he was at the shelter by six.

Nathan had a plan. He needed to look homeless. He went home, hoping that Ginger had not done the laundry yet. He found the hamper still full, so he put on the clothes he wore when he did yard work last week.

In his garage, he found the sneakers he used when playing softball last summer. He'd blown out one of the soles. Since he had overslept this morning, his whiskers had grown some, and finally, he put on a knit cap and his old army overcoat. He would blend in as homeless very well.

It was five forty-five p.m. when he parked his truck four blocks away and walked toward the shelter. He hoped no one spotted him getting out of his truck. As he got closer, he saw several men walking in. He followed them inside and got in line. It was finally his turn at the desk where they all checked in.

"Name, please?" the woman asked.

He didn't want to give his real name. His mind raced, trying to think of what to say. "Joe, Joe Royce." He chuckled in his mind about using Dana's new boyfriend's name.

The woman wrote down his name on a form. "Age?"

"Thirty."

"And, where did you stay last night?"

"I slept in Christopher Columbus Park last night," he replied.

The woman looked up at him. "You know you aren't supposed to sleep in that park."

"Yes, ma'am, but I was there, tired, and didn't feel like walking anywhere else."

"Just be careful. You'll get arrested, if they catch you

there. Do you have an ID?"

"No. I was mugged last week and they took it."

She finished writing on the form and then tore off the bottom part and handed it to him. "Give this to the lady in the cafeteria. Come back tomorrow and we'll see about getting you a new ID."

"Thank you." Nathan took the paper and walked down the hallway, and again found himself in a line, this time for food.

He'd have to remember to send the shelter a donation the next week. He didn't want to take food that someone else needed. He got up to the serving line and picked up a tray. He was given a bowl of beef stew, a biscuit, butter, an apple, and a piece of pie. He stopped to pick up a cup of coffee. He then found a seat at a table that gave him a view of not only the whole room, but also the door to watch for Giles to come in.

A few other men walked over and joined him at the table. "Hello, I'm Jimmy," one of them said.

"I'm Joe. How ya doing?" Nathan replied.

"This is Bob and George."

The men nodded to Nathan.

"I haven't seen you in here before. Where you from?"

"I'm from here in Boston. Just got out of the army a few months ago and can't find a job. There's not much calling out there for a machine gunner," Nathan said.

"It's terrible the way the veterans are treated nowadays," one of the other men said.

"Where do you usually stay?" Jimmy asked.

"Oh, here and there. I had a friend tell me this place was one of the best in town. Maybe you know him. William Giles?"

"Can't say I've heard that name before. Any of you guys?"

The men shook their heads no.

"I haven't seen him in a while and thought I'd stop in here to find him."

"Talk to the lady that was at the table where you came in. She keeps a message board for contacts. If you've got a cell phone, maybe he'll get the message and call you," Jimmy suggested.

"That's a good idea. Thanks." He finished his meal, which was actually pretty good food.

He hadn't seen anyone come in that looked like Giles. It could take days or weeks to find him this way. He took his empty tray over to a window to the kitchen and stacked it on top of the others, and then started to walk back to the door he came in through.

Nathan didn't see the woman from earlier, but he did find another lady in an office near the entrance. "Excuse me, do you know William Giles? I think he sometimes comes in here. He's a friend of mine."

"I'm sorry. The name doesn't sound familiar, but I don't know everyone that comes in here. You can leave a message for him, if you want."

"How do I do that?"

"You write a message on one of these index cards and put it in an envelope. We keep it in a file and post his name on our message board in the hallway. If he sees his name, he comes to the office and we give him the envelope."

"I'd like to do that."

She handed him a card and envelop. He sat a table in the office and wrote his message. *Please call. Urgent.* He signed his real first name and added his cell phone number. He sealed the card in the envelope, wrote Giles name on the front, and handed it to the lady.

She took the envelope and placed it in a file box. "Sometimes, it takes a while for the person to answer, if at all."

"I understand. Thanks."

"Is there anything else we can do for you? Gloves, socks, shoes?" She looked at his feet, specifically his blown-out shoe.

"I'm fine."

"If you need a bed for the night, we have some available."

"No, thanks. I actually prefer staying outside." Nathan left the shelter and walked back to his truck. He took his coat and knit hat off and got in, moving his truck a little closer to the shelter. He wanted to watch for a while, hoping to see Giles go in. He watched for about two hours, never seeing Giles, or if he did, he didn't recognize him in the dark. He finally decided to call it a night.

Chapter Seven

The next morning, after getting the warrant for Bruce Gates' financial records and going over them, Nathan called Gates and scheduled him to come in that afternoon for questioning. He arrived promptly at one p.m. and Nathan took him back to the interrogation room. He read him his rights before starting the questioning.

"I'm surprised you didn't bring an attorney with you today, Mr. Gates."

"I am an attorney, and I've done nothing wrong. I don't need one," Gates replied.

"I understand you were next to Mrs. Blanton's side at Chuck's funeral. Then, you answered the phone when I called her about the coin. Have you two taken up again?"

"No, we haven't. Sarah has no family and needed someone with her at the funeral. I was at her home when you called because I'm handling Chuck's estate."

Nathan wrote some notes down in the file. "I noticed in your financial record that you took out a large sum of money, four thousand dollars, about a year ago. What did you use that for?"

Gates was very careful with his words. "I loaned it to Chuck. You checked my bank accounts?"

" I had a warrant. What did Chuck use the money for?"

"He bought a life insurance policy on himself."

"It was a pretty large policy, from what we understand. Why did he need such a large policy?"

"He told me he'd just had a physical for work, and even though it passed it, the doctor told him he needed to lose weight or he was heading for a heart attack. He didn't think he could lose the weight, and didn't want to leave Sarah penniless, if it happened."

"Did he ever pay you back?" Nathan asked.

"In a matter of speaking."

"Would you explain."

"He had been educating me about his coin collecting. He asked if I'd be interested in taking some of his more valuable coins as payment for the money I loaned him. I was interested and told him that would be fine."

"Is that what he did?"

"Yes."

"What did you do with the coins he gave you?"

"I had them appraised."

"And, how much were they worth?"

"The appraiser said they were valued at around five thousand dollars."

"That's pretty impressive for him to have coins of that value, don't you think?" Nathan asked.

"Not really. He was always talking about how valuable his coins were."

Nathan paused for a minute before asking his next question. "Where were you the night Chuck Blanton was killed?"

"I was home, sleeping."

"Alone?"

"Of course, I was alone."

"So, you don't have an alibi?"

"I suppose I don't," Gates said. "Do I need one?"

"You might. I think we're finished. If I need anything else, I'll let you know."

"I know it looks bad, but I didn't kill him, Detective."

"Thank you for coming in, Mr. Gates." Nathan opened the door, and walked Gates to the front of the building.

Still wanting to find William Giles, Nathan worked late calling more of the homeless shelters in Boston. With so many shelters to call, it would take him days to contact all of them, and he didn't even know if Giles was still in Boston. He could be anywhere in the New England area. After making several calls, he was no closer to finding him. No one had heard of him or admitted to knowing him.

He finally gave up for the night and left for home, but needed to make one stop first. He parked on the street in front of the library to return the coin collecting books he had checked out. Arriving too late, it was closed for the day, but he slipped the books through the book drop slot.

He started back to his truck when he noticed someone lurking in the shadows around a house across the street. He felt for his gun in the holster at the curve of his back. Crouching low, he crossed the street.

Nathan could see the man had something in his hand, so he pulled his gun. With the streetlights on, it made it harder to sneak up on him without being seen. Using the cars to hide behind, he finally approached the person, who was looking into a window. Nathan could see now see that the man held a camera, not a weapon. "Police, don't move!"

The man threw his hands up in the air. Nathan took the camera from his hand and dropped it to the ground, handcuffed him, and spun him around.

"Joe Cassidy? What the hell are you doing here?"

"I'm working a divorce case. Can we move away from the house? I don't want to be seen"

Nathan picked up the camera and walked Joe back to his truck. "Thanks. Now, can you take the cuffs off?"

"Not just yet," Nathan said. He was kind of enjoying having Joe in handcuffs, even if it was only for a short time. "Tell me about this divorce case."

"This wife asked me to follow her husband because she

thought he was having an affair. I followed him here, and you know what, he is having an affair. All I got to do now is get the evidence. That's why I was looking into the window, but you took my camera before I could get any photos. These cuffs are really starting to hurt." He twisted around for Nathan to unlock them. He didn't.

"You're lucky I'm on my way home, or I would arrest you for being a peeping Tom. Turn around." Nathan unlocked the handcuffs, and Joe immediately started rubbing his wrists.

"Thanks. Can I have my camera?" Joe asked.

Before Nathan gave him the camera back, he checked the photos on the card. Finding no shots of the couple inside the house, he handed the camera to him. "Go home, and if you're caught looking into windows like this again, I'll make sure you're arrested. Keep your surveillance to public areas."

"Got it. Thanks." He took his camera, and once in his car, he drove off. Nathan did the same, going home.

He stopped by his mail box to get the day's mail and also the *Mystic Messenger*. Once inside the house, he fixed himself a sandwich and got a beer from the refrigerator. Sitting on the couch, he called Robin while he ate his sandwich.

"Hello, Nathan."

"Good evening. I just got home from work and thought I'd give you a call."

"That's nice. I was just getting ready to get into the tub."

Nathan pictured her wrapped in a white towel, hair pulled up on top of her head, and candles burning around her in a dimly lit bathroom. "Don't let me stop you." He chuckled.

"You're imagining me naked, aren't you?"

"I am, and I like it."

"I'm not even in the bathroom yet."

"I'll wait."

"I'm not having phone sex with you."

"Too bad. How was your day today?" he asked.

"Busy, as usual. Have you turned up anything new on the murder case?"

"Not really." He still hadn't told her about William Giles, so he couldn't mention his venture into the world of the Boston homeless. "The case has kind of stalled. I was hoping you might have turned up something."

"Nothing on my end either."

"Oh, I questioned Bruce Gates today. He said that he loaned Blanton the money for that life insurance policy, and Blanton paid him back with some coins."

"That's interesting. Do you still think Gates and Blanton's wife conspired in the murder?"

"They are pretty strong suspects, but I still don't have any concrete evidence. It's driving me crazy."

"Just keep at it. You'll figure it out. Do you have any plans for the weekend?" she asked.

"Not really. Want to come back down here again?" He hoped she would, so his image of her in the bathtub could become a reality.

"I wish I could, but I'm going to a concert Saturday night with some friends and then to the Pats game on Sunday. Do you want to come?"

"Maybe another time. I better stay close to home this weekend in case something turns up. I'll let you get to your bath. I'll call again soon. Goodnight." He ended the call, took the last drink of his beer, and went to bed.

When Nathan got to work the next morning, he was glad it was Friday. It had been a long week and he was looking forward to doing nothing over the weekend but sleeping. He'd stopped by Ginger's to get his usual large coffee to-go and now sat at his desk looking over his emails.

Officer Ryan Avery stuck his head into Nathan's office. "There's doughnuts in the breakroom. They're still warm." It was an occasional treat paid for by the local Fraternal Order of Police chapter.

Since Nathan had skipped breakfast, doughnuts sounded pretty good right then. He went to get a few before they all disappeared. Most of the patrol officers had gathered in the breakroom to get some of the treats before heading in for their morning briefing.

After choosing his sweet roll, he walked over to see what Hank and Gloria were discussing. "What's the topic of the day?" he asked.

"Tonight's high school football game," Hank said.

"It's Homecoming Night," Gloria added. She was especially excited, since her husband was the head coach. "There's a parade at four p.m. and the game starts at six. You're coming, aren't you?"

"We're playing our rival Gloucester," Hank said. "Remember, how our games used to be, back when?"

Nathan laughed. "They were usually pretty rough."

"Tonight's will probably be about the same. Although, Steve keeps a tight rein on the team."

"I was looking forward to a quiet night at home, but maybe I'll stop by. It sounds like fun," Nathan said. He stopped to get another doughnut and then went back to his office.

About an hour had passed when Nathan's phone rang. The display showed it was Chief Cabot calling from his office. "Perry," he answered.

"Perry, come up to my office right now. I need to talk to you about the murder investigation."

Nathan hung up the phone, took the elevator to the second floor, and rounded the corner to the chief's office.

"Come in, come in."

Nathan sat down.

"Perry, I've left you alone during this investigation long enough. What can you tell me?" the chief asked.

"Well sir, we have several suspects, but not enough evidence on any of them to make an arrest. Honestly, I don't know what to do next. I even went undercover at one of the homeless shelters in Boston this week to see if I could find one of the suspects we haven't talked to yet."

"You---undercover---you went undercover? Did you tell anyone you were doing this?"

Nathan thought the chief was having an aneurysm the way he was acting. "No, sir. I didn't tell anyone. It was a spur of the minute idea at the end of the day."

He sat up in his chair and waved his finger at Nathan. "If you ever do something like that again without telling someone where you're going, you'll be put on suspension. Do you understand?"

"Yes, sir. Got it."

"Good." He sat back. "Did you find the suspect?"

"No. I didn't, but I was able to leave a message for him. If he shows up there, they said they'd have him call me. I've also been calling the other shelters in the city to see if I can find him, but no luck yet. We've also issued a BOLO on him, so other agencies will be watching for him."

"The mayor called me today asking for an update. Apparently, the *Boston Globe* has been running a series about the murder and the mayor is not happy. She's asked you and I to meet her again with the update. I certainly hope you will give a more positive spin on the update than you've given to me here."

"When is the meeting?" Nathan asked.

"Right now. Let's go."

Chief Cabot and Nathan dispensed with driving and walked over to City Hall. Mayor Cranston welcomed them into her office. They all sat down.

"Gentlemen, thank you for coming so quickly. I've been reading several articles in the *Boston Globe* and one in *Boston Magazine* about our murder here in Mystic. While I like it when Mystic gets publicity, I don't like it when we get this type of publicity."

Thank you, Robin, Nathan thought sarcastically.

"No, ma'am. This isn't the impression we want to give about Mystic," the chief said.

"Agreed. So, what can you tell me about making an arrest?" she asked.

"We have several suspects, ma'am," Nathan said.

"How many?" she asked.

"At least four."

"That's a lot, isn't it?"

"Yes, ma'am, but we're working very hard to narrow the list down. I'm sure we'll make some headway soon."

"It sounds like you're sugar-coating it, Detective," the mayor said.

The chief started rubbing his forehead.

"I'm trying not to, ma'am," Nathan said. "The truth is that the investigation has stalled. We have one suspect that we can't seem to find, even though I've gone to great lengths to do so."

"I haven't seen anything in the newspaper or television about a suspect," she said.

"We haven't released that to the media. We don't want to spook him into hiding," Nathan explained.

"It seems to me that he's already in hiding, if you can't find him," the mayor pointed out.

"Yes, ma'am. You're probably right."

"Send out a release to the media today, and see what happens," she ordered.

"I'll start working on that as soon as I get back to my office," Nathan said.

"Very well. You can go, but Chief Cabot, I'd like for you to stay for a few more minutes. I want to talk to you about the street closures for the Homecoming Parade this evening."

Nathan left the mayor's office as quickly as possible. He felt like a scolded child leaving the principal's office. Back at the police department, he didn't think it was a good idea releasing information about William Giles to the press, but if that's what the mayor wanted, he'd do it.

He enlisted Public Information Officer Patterson's help drafting a release to the media saying Giles was a person of interest in the case. Once Patterson got it written, he emailed it to Nathan for approval, and then it went out to all the newspapers and television stations in the area.

Nathan returned from lunch to his voicemail full of messages from several media outlets. He deleted all but one. That one was from Robin and she didn't sound happy. He called her.

"Robin Fisher," she answered.

"Robin, it's Nathan."

Before he could say anything else, she interrupted. "You lied to me. You told me you had nothing new on the case, but you did. Why didn't you tell me about Giles, and why didn't I get this information before you sent it out? I thought we had a deal."

She was clearly upset. "You know as well as I do, I can't release everything I have from the investigation, especially to the press. The mayor ordered me to send the press release out, and I didn't have time to call you. Besides, I've already given you more than I should have, and I'm pretty sure you haven't given me all that you know too."

"Everything I know, you know. Unlike you, I kept my end of the deal."

"What if I promise to give you the exclusive when we finally make the arrest?"

"You'll keep your promise this time?" she asked.

"I will not let any other press know about the arrest until I call you."

"Not even your little girlfriend at the Mystic paper?"

"You will be the first, and she's not my girlfriend. That should be obvious to you." He was getting a little tired of this back and forth between them.

"Okay. So, how close are you to an arrest?" she asked.

"Not close at all. Hopefully, this release will bring us Giles, and we can question him."

"Is he a suspect or just a person of interest, like the press release said?"

He had to do it again. He couldn't tell her the truth just now. "He's a person of interest. He may have seen something the night of the murder, and not realized what he saw. Please don't print that. I don't want to put him in jeopardy, or cause him to not contact us."

"Fine. I won't write that."

"I really need to go. It's a busy day today," he said. "I'll call you this weekend."

"I'm busy this weekend, remember?"

"Right. Well, you call me when you can."

"I will. Bye." She hung up.

At three o'clock that afternoon, Gloria stopped by Nathan's office. "I'm heading out to help with crowd control for the Homecoming parade. Want to come? I bet you could use a break."

"I could, but I better stay here in case something comes in about Giles."

"But, you're coming to the game tonight, aren't you?"

"I'm going to try."

"I'll see you there, then." She headed out.

The rest of the afternoon went pretty slow. The information about Giles would be on the evening news. It was five-thirty and the football game started at six. He really needed to stay to see if anything came in after the news, but it had been a long day. Gloria was right, he needed a break. He closed up his office and drove over to the football game.

As he got near the admission gate, he held his money out to a lady sitting at a desk. "Hello, Detective. I didn't think I'd see you here." It was Mayor Cranston. She took his money.

"You're the last person I thought I'd see tonight too," he said.

"My son plays on the team. He's number eighty-seven."

"I'll look for him." He started to walk ahead.

"I hope I wasn't too hard on you this morning," she said.

"No, ma'am. I should have done that to start."

"Thank you. Enjoy the game."

Nathan walked toward the bleachers, which were packed. Fortunately, he saw Hank just leaving the concession stand. "Hey, I was wondering how I was going to find you in this crowd."

"Yeah, we always have a good turnout, but especially when it's Homecoming," Hank said. "Come on, we have some seats saved."

He followed Hank up the steps of the bleachers until they reached Helen, Hank's wife, who was sitting behind Gloria. Several other people from the police department were there also.

"I'm so glad you could make it tonight," Gloria said.

"I wouldn't have missed it," he told her, and then sat next to Hank.

A few minutes later, Nathan saw Dana climbing up the bleacher steps toward them. She said hello to everyone as she side-stepped down Nathan's row, until she reached him and sat down. "Good evening," she said.

"Hello. How are you this evening?"

"I'm fine. I was a little surprised to see that press release come over my email today. I would have thought you'd have called me personally about it rather than have Officer Patterson send it."

"I wasn't avoiding you. The mayor told me to write up a release, and then Patterson sent it to everyone," Nathan said.

Just then, the Mystic Wizards scored a touchdown. Everyone stood and cheered. After the extra point, everyone sat down again.

"Is there anything else you can tell me about the investigation?"

Good grief, I have got to find someone who is not a reporter to date, he thought to himself. "No, the release had it all. Can we not talk shop tonight? I've been busy with this all day."

"Of course. I'm sorry." Dana got up and side-stepped back down the row, and she ended up sitting next to Helen for the rest of the game.

Hank leaned over to Nathan. "What did you do?"

"Absolutely, nothing."

The home team ended up winning the game, and Dana quickly left, as soon as it was over. Nathan waited with Gloria until her husband came out of the locker room and then he went home.

***

Very early Saturday morning, Nathan's phone rang. He pulled himself out of a deep sleep to answer. "Hello."

"Detective Perry, this is Officer Patterson. Detective Perry, are you there?"

"What? Yes, I'm here." Nathan sat up on the side of his bed.

"Detective, the phone here has been ringing off the hook since that story was on the news last night. The lieutenant told me to call you to come in and help with the calls. Detective?"

"I heard you. I'll be right there." He hung up. Looking at the clock, he realized it was only seven a.m. *Too damn early*, he thought. He stumbled to the bathroom and into the shower. Twenty minutes later, he was out the door on the way to the police department, but not without stopping first for his usual morning coffee to-go at Ginger's.

Once at the PD, he went to Patterson's office, finding him on the phone. He sat down and waited.

"Thank you for your call." Patterson hung up and looked up at Nathan. "The night officer in charge was not happy with all the calls overnight. I got here at six and started right in." His phone rang. "It's been non-stop since I got here. Lieutenant Matthews said to have you come in to help. Sorry." He picked up the phone. "Mystic PD, can I help you?"

After Patterson ended that call, he handed Nathan a stack of messages. I'll keep with the calls, if you can go over these to see if any of them are worth checking out."

Nathan took the messages. "Sure, if you need a break, let me know, and I'll take some of the calls. I'll be in my office," he said, as the phone rang again. He went to his office and

124

started going through the messages. He made two piles: one for the unsubstantiated calls, and one for the trash can.

Around nine o'clock, Nathan took over the calls for Patterson. A few of the messages looked promising for finding William Giles. He put those in a file. Then, by noon, the calls had slowed down enough for the regular switchboard to handle them.

Nathan made sure there was an officer available in case they got overwhelmed again, and then he went home. So much for a quiet weekend. Although, the rest of the weekend was relatively calm.

By the beginning of the workday on Monday, Nathan was at his desk looking through the messages that came in after he left on Saturday, and more that called on Sunday. Only a handful looked like something that would need to be investigated more. He prioritized all the messages from most important to least, and he hoped he could get a few other officers to assist in investigating them further.

A knock at his door drew his attention to Mallory standing there. "Are you busy?" she asked.

"Yes, but I need a break. Please, come in."

"I have some news. I emailed you three videos, but since I didn't hear back from you, I thought I'd make sure you got them."

"I haven't even opened my email program this morning. I started right in on these messages from the weekend."

"I heard the phones were busy all weekend."

Nathan opened his email program, and then the email that she had sent. "What did you send me?"

For the past few weeks, I've been going through photos and videos that people have sent in that were taken at the coin convention. I found two that I thought you should see. She moved behind Nathan so she could see the screen. "Open that one first," she said, pointing to one of the attachments.

"I don't understand what I'm supposed to be seeing." Nathan said.

"This is cell phone video taken of someone buying a coin from a vendor. Look in the background at the end of the row. See those two people talking to each other?" she said.

Nathan looked closer. "That's Alex Gold, isn't it? Who is she talking to?"

"Open the second attachment."

He clicked on it and it was the same video, except it had been edited to zoom in on the two people talking. Gold was talking to Chuck Blanton, but not just talking. They were arguing with each other. "Would you look at that ... I wish we could hear what they're saying."

"There's no way to get the audio of it, but it does look like they're in a heated discussion."

"When was this taken?"

"This was the day before he was murdered," she replied.

"Nice work, Mallory. What's this last video?"

"I had gone through the video from the hotel surveillance system of the convention hall earlier and didn't notice anything. However, after we got a photo of William Giles, I went over it again, and found him."

Nathan clicked on the last video and watched closely.

"That's Giles right there," Mallory said. "I edited it together and it shows that Giles was following Blanton around the convention hall on that same day. At the end of the video, it shows him briefly talking to Blanton, and then Giles leaves."

"I'm very impressed with your work, Mallory. You've showed some real dedication. I can't even begin to tell you how much I appreciate what you've done. Thank you."

She blushed. "It's all in a day's work."

"I'm definitely going to write a letter of appreciation for your personnel file."

"That's nice. Thanks. What are you going to do now?" she asked.

"I'm going to see if I can find out from Alex Gold what she and Blanton were arguing about."

"Do you think she'll tell you?"

"She better. She just bumped her way up the suspect list."

Mallory went back to her office, and Nathan picked up the phone and called Sam Denzinger at the State Police office in Boston.

"Detective Denzinger."

"Sam, its Nathan Perry."

"How are you, Nathan?"

"I'm pretty good. I hope I didn't catch you at a busy time. I have a favor to ask."

"Actually, I am a little busy. What do you need?"

"I have to interview Alex Gold again. She has an office in Boston, and I was hoping you could go with me today."

Denzinger let out a deep breath. "If you can wait about three hours, I can make it."

"That would work out perfectly. I'll meet you at your office."

"See you then," Denzinger said.

Nathan had to prepare everything for his questioning of Alex Gold. He went to Mallory's office to get a few things.

Three hours later, Nathan walked into Denzinger's office. "Good afternoon."

Denzinger stood and shook hands. "What's new with your case?" he asked.

Nathan showed him the video of Miss Gold and Blanton arguing.

"That is interesting."

"This happened the day before the murder, and Alex never mentioned anything about them arguing when we talked to her."

"We better get going, or she'll wonder where we are," Denzinger said.

"Oh, she doesn't know we're coming. I didn't want to tell her or she might not be there. She really doesn't like talking to me."

When they arrive at Miss Gold's office, they encountered

her secretary first. "Hello. May I help you?" she asked.

Nathan showed his badge, as did Denzinger. "I'm Nathan Perry of the Mystic Police Department, and this is Detective Denzinger from the State Police. We'd like to speak with Alex Gold."

The sight of the badges seemed to shake the secretary. She fumbled her words as she spoke. "Miss Gold isn't here, and ah, I'm not sure when she'll be back."

"Are you sure she isn't here? I thought I saw her car in the parking garage," Nathan said.

"No, I mean yes. She's not here."

Just then the door to an office opened up and Alex Gold stepped out. Both men looked at Miss Gold and then at the secretary.

"She must have just got here," Nathan said, somewhat sarcastically.

"It's okay, Gabby. Hello, Detective Perry. What do you need now?" Alex said.

"You remember Detective Denzinger from the State Police. We'd like a moment of your time."

"A moment is about all I have. Come into my office," she said.

The two men followed her in and they all sat down around her desk. Nathan got out the computer tablet that he brought with him. "I'd like for you to look at a video we have." She kept a very stoic face while watching.

The video finished and she looked up. "So?"

"So? What were you and Blanton arguing about?" Nathan asked.

She picked up a cigarette and lit it. "I don't really remember." She took a puff and blew smoke in their direction.

"You can answer my question here today, or I can make you come to the police department with your lawyer and answer them there. Your choice, and I know how much you hate coming to Mystic."

"Fine." She put her cigarette down in an ashtray.

"Blanton had just told me that he was pulling his coin out of the auction. I told him that I had already advertised the coin and had several bidders coming in specifically for that coin. He would ruin my reputation if that coin wasn't in the auction. I told him I would sue him."

"What did he say to that?" Denzinger asked.

"He said he didn't care. He had another buyer that was going to pay him more for it than he would probably get at the auction. So, I threw him out of the convention."

"Did he leave?" Nathan asked.

"I guess so. I didn't see him after that."

"We will be confirming that he didn't come back."

"Go ahead. I hope this is the last time we have to go through all of this. I'm getting rather tired of it."

The two men got up. "We'll be in touch," Nathan said, and then they left.

Outside of the building, Nathan and Denzinger stood for a few minutes before going to their car.

"Do you believe her?" Denzinger asked.

"I actually do, but I definitely want to check it out anyway," Nathan replied.

Chapter Eight

On the way back to Mystic, Nathan wanted to stop in Chelsea, about halfway between the two towns. One of the phone calls over the weekend claimed to be a relative of William Giles, and that needed to be investigated further.

He found the home and knocked on the door. An older man answered.

Nathan showed his badge. "I'm Detective Perry from the Mystic Police Department. Did you call about William Giles over the weekend?"

"Yes, I did. Come in." He opened the screen door allowing Nathan to come in and follow him to the dining room where they sat down at the table. "I'm Gerald Giles, Will's older brother."

"Thank you for calling us. Do you know where we can find him?"

"Did he kill that guy from Boston?" Mr. Giles asked, wearily.

"We're not sure, but he may know something that could help us figure out who did. He may not even realize that he knows something."

"He was always in trouble when he was a kid. He ran around with the wrong bunch of boys when we lived in Worcester. After we moved here to Chelsea, he got his act together and mostly stayed out of trouble."

"Does he still live around here?" Nathan asked.

"No. After he graduated from high school, he left for Boston. He wanted to live in the big city. We didn't hear from him much after he left. He only occasionally came home for a visit."

"When was the last time you saw him?"

"Oh, it's probably been over a year, but I recognized his picture when they showed it on TV."

"Do you happen to know where he lives now?"

"I have an old address for him in Boston, but I don't know if he lives there anymore. Let me get that." He got up and went through a drawer in the kitchen. He finally found an address book, and brought it back to the table. "This is all I have." He showed Nathan a page in the book.

Nathan snapped a picture of it with his phone. "Mr. Giles, I really appreciate you contacting us about your brother. This is my card. If William should contact you, please tell him to call me. We just need to talk to him."

"I'll do that. I feel bad for that man's family. If Will knows something, I'm sure he'll do the right thing."

Nathan left and headed back to Mystic. As soon as he got back to the police department, he called his contact at the Boston Police Department to have them check on the address he'd obtained for Giles. The officer told him he'd get back to him as soon as they knew something.

After lunch, Nathan went through more phone messages that came in while he was gone when his cell phone rang. "Hello, Robin. How was the concert over the weekend?"

"It was great. How was your weekend?"

"Not as restful as I had hoped."

"I'm sorry to hear that. I have something you may be interested in."

"What's that?" He sat back in his chair.

"My source was able to get me a copy of Blanton's life insurance policy."

"I don't suppose you're ready to tell me who your source

is?"

"You know I can't do that. I noticed something about Blanton's signature on the policy. I don't think he's the one that signed it," she said.

"Really?" Nathan moved closer to his desk and made a note on a pad of paper. "Why do you think that?"

"I'm no expert, but it seems like there is a jerkiness or hesitation in the signature. I was hoping that you might have his real signature and could compare it."

"I'm sure we have his signature on something. Can you email it to me? I'll check with our evidence technician to see what we have."

I'll do that right now."

As he waited for Robin's email, he emailed Mallory, asking her for a copy of Blanton's signature from any evidence found in his hotel room.

Ding. "I just got your email." He opened it and the attachment. "You only sent me the signature. How about the whole policy?"

"In due time. In due time," she teased.

"I spoke to a relative of William Giles today."

"How did you find a relative?"

"He saw the story about him on the news and called in. He said he doesn't know where he is, but had an old address for him in Boston. The PD there is checking on it for me."

"I don't suppose I could have the relative's name, could I?"

"In due time. In due time." They both laughed.

Ding. "I just got the copy of Blanton's signature from evidence. Hmmm, they look pretty similar. I really can't tell if they were written by the same person, or not. Let me send them to the State Police. I'm sure they have a handwriting expert that can look at them. When I get the results, I'll send you a copy."

"You promise?"

"I do promise. Thanks for the info."

"Call me, if you make it up to Boston again."

"I will. Bye."

They ended the call. He put his cell phone down, and picked up his desk phone to place a call.

"Detective Denzinger."

"Sam, it's Nathan."

"So, soon? I just saw you this morning."

"I just got some info that I need checked. Does the State Police have a handwriting expert?"

"Yes, we do. What have you got?"

"I just got a copy of Blanton's signature from that big life insurance policy he had. The person that sent it to me doesn't think it's his signature. I also have a copy of his signature from something found in his hotel room after his murder. Can I email them to you to have your expert check?"

"Absolutely. I'll take it to him myself."

"Thanks. I'll get it to you in a few minutes. Thanks.

"You're welcome."

He hung up the receiver and started typing on his computer to get the email sent to Denzinger.

That night, Nathan had a restless sleep, tossing and turning all night. He finally got up at six a.m. After a shower, he decided to go to the Witch's Brew for breakfast before work. It wasn't even daylight yet when he walked in. Only a few people were there, so he had his choice of tables, but he took his usual booth near the counter.

Ginger brought him a cup of coffee. "Good morning, handsome."

Nathan laughed. "Good morning."

"You actually look like hell. Bad night?"

"I couldn't sleep. Would you bring me scrambled eggs, hashbrowns, and a slice of ham?"

"Coming up."

Ding-a-ling. Nathan heard the door, but didn't look to see who came in. He'd brought his newspaper with him and was concentrating on it.

"Mind if I join you?"

He looked up. It was Dana. "I don't mind at all. You sure you want to sit with me?"

"Yes. I need to apologize." She took her coat off and sat down on the other side of the booth. "I'm so sorry about how I acted at the football game. It was childish of me to move to another seat."

"Forget it. I already have," he said.

Ginger walked up with a cup of coffee for Dana. "What can I get you for breakfast?"

"I'll take a veggie omelet this morning."

"It'll just be a minute," Ginger said, turning for the kitchen.

"Thanks," Dana replied, then looked back at Nathan. "Anything new on the investigation?"

"We were overrun with phone calls after the TV stations in Boston ran the story about Giles. I'm surprised our system didn't crash."

"Can I print that?" she asked.

"Sure."

"Did you get any good leads?"

"I'm following up on a few, but nothing I can talk specifically about yet," he said.

Ginger brought their breakfast. "Can I get you two anything else?"

"I think we're good," Nathan said, and she left. He grabbed the catsup bottle and squirted some on his hash browns and eggs.

"How can you eat that with catsup on it?" Dana asked.

"Hashbrowns are just potatoes. You eat it on French Fries, don't you?"

"Well, yes, but not on eggs."

Nathan laughed and finished his breakfast, while Dana did the same. Ginger brought their checks and Nathan's usual large coffee to-go. They paid their bills, and walked out together.

"If anything else comes up in your investigation, you'll let me know?" Dana asked.

"You'll be my first call." She left smiling. He felt bad, knowing that his first call would actually be to Robin, but his second would be to Dana.

Nathan didn't like that the investigation was at a standstill. There were too many suspects, and not enough evidence. Something had to change. Maybe he needed to brainstorm the case with the other officers involved. If everything was discussed out loud, something might pop out to them.

He picked up his office phone and called Gloria, hoping she was at her post this morning.

"Good morning, Nathan," she answered.

"Good morning. I'm going to get several officers together around one p.m. in the briefing room to go over Blanton's case and I'd like for you to be there."

"I'll be there."

"Thanks." He hung the phone up and called Hank, asking him the same thing. He also agreed. One last call was to Sam Denzinger.

"Sam, is there any way you can make it down here around one o'clock for a meeting to brainstorm the Blanton case?" Nathan asked.

"I wish I could, but I'm buried under cases of my own today. However, I'll be by my desk, if you need anything during the meeting."

"Thanks."

"Hey, while I've got you on the phone. Our handwriting expert took a look at those signatures you sent me."

"What was the result?"

"He said they were definitely not signed by the same person."

"Just as we thought. Could he send me a statement certifying that?" Nathan asked.

"He's supposed to write it up today and I'll get it to you as soon as possible."

"Thanks, Sam. That's a big help."

Nathan spent the rest of the morning making charts of the evidence for each suspect. At ten a.m., he decided he needed a break. He got a soda from the break room and walked back to his office. He ran into Chief Cabot in the hallway.

"Perry, anything new on the murder investigation?"

"Unfortunately, no. However, I'm planning a brainstorming session today at one o'clock in the briefing room. If you'd like to attend, your thoughts would be welcomed."

"That sounds like a good idea. You know who might also be interested is Mayor Cranston. I'll give her a call to see if she can attend." Seemingly pleased with himself, the chief headed back to his office.

Nathan was not thrilled that the mayor might be in attendance at the meeting, but there was nothing he could do about it now. Back in his office, he made one more call to make that he forgot earlier. "Mallory, I'm having a meeting at one o'clock in the briefing room about the Blanton case. Can you make it?"

"I think I can."

"Great. See you then."

He finished with the charts and took them into the room to prepare for the meeting. A little before one, the officers started coming in. Also attending was Sergeant Donnelly and Lieutenant Matthews. Lastly, Chief Cabot entered the room with Mayor Cranston. Nathan walked over to greet the mayor.

"Good afternoon, Mayor. It's nice that you could come today."

"Thank you, Detective. I was intrigued when your chief called and invited me."

"One thing before we begin. This is still an active investigation, and as such, anything discussed here today has to remain confidential. You can talk to anyone else about this." Nathan hoped he had approached this subject gently enough.

"I completely understand. Nothing will leave here."

"Thank you, ma'am." Nathan moved to the front of the room to begin. "Thanks for attending today. I also asked Detective Denzinger from the State Police to be here, but he said he was too busy to be able to leave his office. He still offered his assistance with anything we might need, though. I also asked our prosecutor, Daniel Grant, to join us, but he had court."

"You seem to have a lot of suspects up there," Chief Cabot said.

"Yes, sir. That's the problem. I plan on going over all of the suspects, and as you can see, I have listed the evidence we have under each of their names. Everything so far is circumstantial, and not enough for an arrest to be made on anyone."

"You can't make an arrest based on circumstantial evidence?" the mayor asked.

"We can, but even that evidence is pretty thin at this time," Nathan replied. "Our first suspect is Sarah Blanton, the victim's wife. Just today, Detective Denzinger told me that the State Police handwriting expert has determined the signature on a five-hundred-thousand-dollar life insurance policy is not that of the victim. The beneficiary of that policy is Mrs. Blanton."

"That's a good motive right there," Sergeant Donnelly said.

"It is. If she did it, she may have had an accomplice. Mr. Blanton's friend and attorney, Bruce Gates, was having an affair with Mrs. Blanton that ended a few months before the murder. He's my second suspect. They both say the affair ended, but in my option, I think they've taken up again."

"They sure looked cozy to me when I was at Blanton's funeral," Gloria added.

"The third suspect is William Giles. Our evidence technician, Mallory Duncan, found Giles on the hotel surveillance video following Blanton around the coin show the day of the murder. Hank also talked to a few people that saw Giles in the bar that evening when Blanton was there also."

"That's right," Hank said. "The bartender out there said he was watching Blanton in the bar that night and left just a little while after Blanton was told to leave, after he'd had a little too much to drink, and was arguing with some of the other collectors."

"We also got an overwhelming amount of phone calls after the story about Giles being a person of interest was on the television news. I spoke to Giles' brother, and he gave me an old address for him in Boston. The PD up there checked on that and he no longer lived there, but they're keeping an eye out for him in the neighborhood. Our last suspect is the convention organizer, Alex Gold. Blanton was supposed to have auctioned off a rare coin at the convention, then pulled it from the auction at the last minute. She wasn't happy about that. Mallory did a bang-up job and found Blanton and Alex arguing in the background of a cell phone video that someone submitted to us."

The chief whispered something to the mayor, who then looked in Mallory's direction.

"So that's pretty much it. Anyone have any suggestions on what to do next?" Nathan asked.

"What about the coin that he was going to auction off? Where is it?" the mayor asked.

"No one has it. I did talk to someone at an auction house in Boston that said Blanton showed him cell phone photos of it, but that's about it," Nathan said.

"Did you ever find that cell phone from his employer?" Mallory asked.

"You know, the employer never got back to me on that," Nathan replied. "I'll have to follow up on that. Thank you, Mallory." He made a note of that.

"Money seems to be the best motive and a half-a-million dollars is a lot of money. I think the wife did it," Mayor

Cranston said.

"I agree that money is likely the reason for the murder, but I've been told that the coin Blanton wanted to auction could have gone for as high as three-million dollars," Nathan said. "That could bring either William Giles or Alex Gold in as the murderer."

"Have you looked into everyone's financial records?" the chief asked.

"Everyone except for Giles and Alex Gold," Nathan replied.

"I think that should be your next step then. Someone is going to profit from this murder, and if that much money is involved, they aren't going to want to wait for it. They're going to want it now," Cabot said.

"You're right about the money. I'll see if I can get a warrant for their financial information," Nathan said. "Does anyone have anything else?"

"What about pawn shops in Boston?" Gloria asked. "We got the tip about Giles from a pawn shop owner here in Mystic. If someone has that coin, but doesn't realize the real value of it, they might take it to a pawn shop to sell."

"That's an excellent thought," Nathan said. "With the chief's permission, perhaps some of us could visit pawn shops in Boston looking for the coin, or someone who may have come in wanting to sell a coin."

"You have my permission," Cabot said.

"I have one more suggestion," Gloria said. "If Giles is homeless, he probably doesn't have a financial record to check. He wouldn't have any money. However, if he stole the coin, and sold it, his money problems could be solved. I think he needs to be bumped up on the suspect list."

"That's a very good point, Officer Wheeler. Good job," Chief Cabot said.

Gloria just beamed with pride at the chief's comment.

"Excellent. I think we have our next tasks at hand then. Thank you all for coming, and helping with this," Nathan said.

He was happy to see Gloria coming along as an officer, and even as an investigator.

After the meeting, Gloria, Hank, and Sergeant Donnelly waited around for their assignments. "Gloria, can you get me a list of pawn shops in Boston? I'll divide them up between the four of us. I'll also get a copy of what the coin looks like so you can take it with you when you go." They all headed in different directions. "Sergeant Donnelly, could I have a moment?"

"Yes."

"I just wanted to tell you that I really appreciate you helping with this. I'm sure there are a lot of pawn shops in Boston, and having another officer helping will make a big difference."

"No problem. When I helped you with the arrest of Mayor Newcomb last time, it was like I was a police officer again, rather than the desk jockey I've become, since becoming a sergeant."

"I understand completely. Thanks again."

Nathan went back to his office to call Blanton's employer about his work cell phone.

"Massachusetts Bay Transportation Authority"

"Douglas Wells, please," Nathan requested.

A few minutes later, he came on the line. "This is Douglas Wells. Can I help you?"

"Mr. Wells, this is Detective Perry from the Mystic Police Department. I called you some time ago about the cell phone that Chuck Blanton used while working. Were you ever able to locate it?"

"Yes. Mrs. Blanton just brought it in last week."

"Mrs. Blanton brought it in? She had it?"

"Yes. She said she found it in his lunchbox at home."

Nathan thought that was interesting, since she told him she didn't know where it was. "Have you done anything with the phone, like erase anything on it?"

"No. You told me not to," Wells said.

"Good. Please keep it secured, where no one can have access to it until I can get up there to pick it up."

"I keep it locked in my desk and I have the only key."

"I'm probably going to be in Boston this week. I'll call you when I know for sure, and arrange a time for me to get it."

"That will be fine, just let me know."

"Thank you, Mr. Wells."

That afternoon, Gloria walked into Nathan's office with a stack of printed papers. "Here is the list of pawn shops in Boston," she said, handing him the papers.

"That's a lot of pawn shops."

"There's more than I thought there would be."

"We'll tackle as many of them as we can," Nathan said. "I don't suppose you have divided them up in geographical areas?"

"I did. It wouldn't be much use not to do that."

"Gloria, you never cease to amaze me. You're always a step ahead."

"There's one other thing. As I was researching the pawn shops, I found that there are also coin shops in Boston, a lot of them." She handed him another set of papers, a little smaller.

"These need to be checked also," he said.

"That's what I thought too."

"Would you ask Hank and Sergeant Donnelly to meet us in my office at four o'clock today?"

"Yes, sir." She headed back to her desk.

Nathan then called Douglas Wells back to arrange a time on Wednesday to pick up Blanton's work cell phone. Since he was going to be in Boston, he also called Robin.

"Hi, Nathan," she answered.

"I'm going to be in Boston tomorrow. How about meeting for lunch?"

"Let me check my schedule. I think I'm available." He could hear her shuffling papers. "Yes, I can do lunch tomorrow. What time and where?"

"I'm going to be on the east side of town. Do you know any good places in that area?"

"How about the Marketplace Café on Meridian? They have a pretty good lunch menu."

"Sounds great. I'll see you there around noon."

Nathan ended the call and started looking through the list of shops that Gloria had brought him. This was going to be more difficult than he had thought.

He then had an idea. He actually couldn't believe he was going to act on it, but he needed help. He headed up to see Chief Cabot.

"Come in, Perry. What do you need?" the chief said.

"Well, sir. In the gathering of the list of pawn shops in Boston, we found there's a lot of them, and we also found that there are actually a lot of shops that deal specifically in coins. So many of them that it would take days for the four of us to check all of the shops. With Halloween coming up, and the town having so many more tourists, I would hate to pull another officer off their regular duty to help us, so I was wondering if I could enlist the help of Joe Cassidy to visit some of the shops?" Saying those words actually put a vile taste in his mouth.

The chief sat there, rocking in his chair for several seconds, thinking. "I think that's a great idea. Give him a call and see if he's available."

"Yes, sir. I'll go call him now." Nathan left the chief's office and went back to his. He still couldn't believe he was going to do it, but he needed help. How bad could Joe be? All he had to do was ask about a specific coin. He found Joe's card and dialed his number.

"Joe Cassidy Investigations."

Nathan suspected Joe still didn't have a secretary since he answered his own phone. "Joe, it's Nathan Perry."

"Nathan, I've been meaning to call you. I wanted to thank you again for not arresting me in the other night. I really appreciate it."

"I knew you meant no harm. You just need to make sure you aren't breaking any laws when you're working a case. Listen, I was calling you to see if you might be available to give the police department some assistance in a case."

"Really? You're asking me to help you on another case? Of course, I'm available. What can I do?"

Nathan wasn't surprised at Joe's enthusiasm. "I need an additional person to go to Boston to check some of the pawn shops up there to see if anyone has come in to sell a rare coin."

"This is for the murder case, isn't it? Wow, I guess you really liked my help on your last murder case, eh?"

"Joe, can you do it, or not? I'll need you tomorrow."

"I said I could, didn't I?"

"Yes, I guess you did. Can you come to my office this afternoon around four o'clock? I'll be distributing the list of shops for everyone to check."

"I'll be there, Nathan. Thank you so much." Joe hung up, and Nathan already regretted it.

A little before four o'clock, Gloria came into Nathan's office with Joe Cassidy walking behind her. She leaned down to whisper to Nathan. "Joe said he's here to help us in Boston tomorrow."

"It's a long story," Nathan said.

Joe sat down and Gloria took a seat away from him. A few minutes later, Hank and Sergeant Donnelly came in and sat also. They both looked at Cassidy, and then at Nathan.

"Before we begin, while Gloria was making the list of pawn shops, she discovered that there were several coin shops in Boston also. These shops are just as important, if not more important to check out. Because of the additional shops to check, I've asked Joe Cassidy for assistance. He's going to take a section of the city to check," Nathan explained. "The chief approved this."

"I'm sure I can pull an officer off patrol to help us, so we don't have to have a private citizen involved in this," Donnelly said.

Cassidy looked at Donnelly. It was obvious that he didn't like that comment.

"I already thought of that, but we really need every officer on patrol this time of the year," Nathan said. "Joe, you understand this is a murder investigation. Every reporter out there is looking for information on what we're doing. You cannot talk to anyone outside of the department about what you're doing."

"But, that's just right now. After you catch the guy, I can tell people about how I helped, right?"

Nathan rubbed his forehead. "Yes, Joe. After we solve the murder, you can tell." Nathan passed out the store assignments, a photo of William Giles, and a photo of the coin. "I'll check the coin shops, and have divided the rest of the stores up into districts for each of you to check. Gloria will take the south, Sergeant Donnelly---"

"For the sake of this, you all can call me Shane," Donnelly said.

"Shane?"

"My parents were very Irish," he replied.

"Okay, Shane will take the west side, Joe will take the north, and Hank will check the east side of town. Ask if anyone has come in wanting to sell a Brasher Doubloon. This is a picture of the coin." He held up the photo. "Then, ask if they know the man in the other photo, William Giles. If they've had dealings with him, we need as much information about Giles that they can give. Any questions?"

Cassidy raised his hand.

"Joe."

"If we get information about Giles, should we follow up on it. Like if they have an address, should we go check it out?"

"No," they all said in unison.

"If you get any information about Giles at all, Joe, call my cell phone." Nathan handed him a card.

"Got it."

"If there are no more questions, that's it. Get an early start tomorrow, and call me at the end of the day to report in. Thanks."

They all got up to leave, but the three officers waited until Cassidy left, then looked at Nathan. "You actually asked Cassidy to help?" Hank said.

"Basically, he's harmless, and we really do need every officer here to handle the tourists in town for Halloween festivities."

They all turned to leave. "I hope you know what you're doing," Donnelly said as he went out the door.

The next day in Boston, Nathan first four stops at coins shops proved uneventful. No one had been there trying to sell a Brasher Doubloon. However, at the fifth shop, he got a hit.

He showed his badge and said, "I'm Detective Perry from the Mystic Police Department. I'm looking for someone who might have stopped in here trying to sell a rare Brasher Doubloon coin.

"Yes, someone was in here a few weeks ago asking about selling that coin," the shop owner said.

"Did this person have the coin when he was in here?

"No, he only asked if we would be interested in buying it."

Nathan showed him the photo of Giles. "Can you tell me if this was the man?"

The owner stared at the picture. "No, I don't think that was him."

"Can you tell me what he looked like?"

"I really can't remember what he looked like, but I know this wasn't him."

Nathan looked up and saw a surveillance camera above the counter. "Would you have him on your surveillance video?"

"No," the owner said.

"No? How do you know?"

"Since you're with the police, I guess its okay to tell you. We only use that camera after we close at night in the event of a burglary. We respect the privacy of our customers."

Nathan let out a breath. "What did you tell this man about buying the coin?"

"I told him we didn't have the kind of money that the Doubloon was worth, and suggested he go to an auction house where the bids might go that high."

"Did you mention a specific auction house to him?"

"No, I didn't."

"Thanks for your help," Nathan said.

He moved on to the next coin shop several blocks away, but came up with nothing. At the shop after that, the owner did have video to look at, but the man had a hat on and never turned toward the camera. There was no way to identify him. Nathan had the shop owner email the video to him anyway.

By now, it was close to noon, and Nathan had just enough time to make it to the café to meet Robin for lunch. She was already there when he arrived. He kissed her on the cheek, and sat down. He beat her to the punch by asking first. "Anything new on your investigation?"

"My source gave me the name of the life insurance agent that sold Blanton the policy."

"That's fantastic. What's the name?"

"Hold on. I'm not quite ready to share that yet," she said.

"I thought we had a deal."

"You didn't tell me about Giles before it went out in a press release. That kind of broke our deal."

Nathan sat back in his chair. "I thought we already resolved this issue."

"Let me interview this person first. After that, I'll give you the name."

"Who is this source of yours? It seems that the only info you're getting from them is about the life insurance. It's someone at the insurance company, isn't it?" he asked.

"It's not someone from the insurance company. What

are you doing in Boston?" she asked, changing the subject.

"Myself and a few others are checking pawn shops in town to see if anyone has tried to sell that coin." He didn't mention to her that he was also checking coin shops. If she could keep some information, so could he.

"Any results yet?"

"None of them have called me, so I guess not. I do have one little piece of information for you though. The State Police handwriting expert determined that the signature you sent me was not Blanton's."

"That's big," she said.

"It is. Can you send me the whole copy of the policy now?"

"I suppose I could. I'll get it to you later today."

After lunch, Nathan said goodbye to Robin, giving her a hug and a kiss, and then headed to the Massachusetts Bay Transporation Authority office. He walked up to the window in the lobby.

"Can I help you?" the lady behind the window asked.

He held up his badge. "I'm Detective Perry, here to see Douglas Wells. He's expecting me."

The lady made a call. "He'll be with you in a moment," she told Nathan.

A few minutes later, the door to the lobby opened. "Detective Perry, I'm Douglas Wells. If you'll come with me." He led Nathan down a hallway and into an office. "Please sit down."

"I appreciate you turning over the phone without me having to get a warrant for it."

"Chuck was one of our favorite employees. We want to do anything we can to help." He opened a desk drawer and handed Nathan the phone.

"Has anyone looked in the phone?"

"No one here has. As I told you on the phone, his wife brought it in to us, so I can't guarantee she didn't look through it before she gave it to me."

Nathan took the phone, and put it in an evidence bag, labeling it with his pen. He then handed Wells a reciept for the phone. "We'll return it as soon as we can. Did Chuck have a desk or locker here?"

"He worked security at one of our underground subway stations. He would have had a locker at that station. I really don't know if anyone has done anything with it or not. Let me check." He picked up the phone and made a call. When he hung up, he had an answer. "The security guard at that station said no one has opened Chuck's locker. If you want to go there, I'll let them know you're coming, and they will cut the lock off."

"I would like that, but please tell them not to cut the lock until I get there."

"Of course." He wrote something down on a piece of paper and handed it to Nathan. "Here's the address of the station."

"Thank you, Mr. Wells. I do appreciate your cooperation."

Nathan left the building. When he arrived, he asked the first security person he saw about the locker. He was taken to their on-site supervisor, who took him to Blanton's locker. A maintenance worker was there waiting with bolt cutters to remove the lock. He was given the okay, and it snapped right off.

Nathan opened the locker, and began taking everything out, one item at a time, placing them in a brown paper bag. He found a uniform, pair of shoes, batteries, some coin collecting magazines and books, and finally, a spiral notebook. He glanced through it, and found some handwritten notes about some coins. He added that to the bag and taped it shut, writing his initials over the tape.

"Thank you. I have what I need," he said, and went back to his car. He called Hank. "Did you find anything today?"

"No. No one has come in to sell any Doubloons, and no one recognized Giles' photo," Hank replied.

"You might as well head home to beat the rush hour

traffic then." He then called Gloria, Donnelly, and Cassidy. They all had the same reply as Hank. He told them to head home also, and meet at his office around four p.m.

Chapter Nine

After Nathan reached the police department, he took the evidence from the day to Mallory to log in. He placed it on the shelf attached to the door of cage.

"Hi, Nathan. What do you have?" She came to the door.

"More evidence for the Blanton case. The sack holds the contents of his locker at the subway station where he worked, and this is his work cell phone. Make sure you check the phone card for anything that's been deleted, and could you also check it for fingerprints. I'm sure several people have touched it, but we might get lucky. I'm also going to email you a video when I get to my office. Would you pull a photo off of the customer with the long hair? I'm going to need that photo at my office by four o'clock."

She turned around and looked at the clock on her wall. "I should be able to do that by then."

Nathan went his office and emailed the video to her first thing. He couldn't help but think that he had seen that guy before, but couldn't place where. Thirty minutes later, his thoughts were interrupted when Hank, Gloria, and Donnelly came in and sat down for their meeting. They waited on Cassidy, who was late, but showed up a few minutes later.

Nathan first asked if anyone had come up with anything, hoping someone had turned something up after he had spoken to them on the phone, but no one had. The three officers gave their lists and photos back to Nathan, who then looked at Cassidy for his.

"I left my stuff at my office. Sorry, I can bring it to you tomorrow," Cassidy said.

"Damn it, Joe. That stuff is considered evidence. I told you to keep it with you."

It was then that Mallory showed up at his door. "I'm sorry to interrupt, but you wanted this photo as soon as I could get it." She handed him the photo.

"Thanks." Before he continued, he turned to Cassidy. "Joe, thanks for your help today. I'll stop by your office tomorrow and pick up the items from today." He got up and urged Cassidy to the door, closing it behind him. "He doesn't need to hear any of this." He sat back down behind his desk.

"Could Gloria look at that photo first? I want to see what she thinks about the guy in it," Mallory asked.

Nathan handed the photo to Gloria, who took a long look at it. Then, it was like a lightbulb went off. "That's the guy who owns the pawn shop here in Mystic," she exclaimed.

"That's what I thought too," Mallory said.

Nathan looked through the Blanton file. "James Bass."

"That's his name," Gloria said.

"I think I know that name," Donnelly said. "Did you check for a record on him?"

"No, I didn't." Nathan started typing on his computer.

"There's more," Mallory said. "I checked the card in the cell phone, and I did find two photos had been deleted. They were of coins." She handed him two photos.

"These are Doubloons," Nathan said.

"I have one last thing," she added. "I found a fingerprint on the screen of that flip phone you said was Blanton's. I don't think it's his print, but I sent a scan of the print to the State Police to see if we can get a match on somebody. I hope to know something tomorrow."

"You've done a fantastic job, Mallory. Do you have anything else?" he said.

"No, that's it."

"Thanks." Nathan looked back at his computer. "Bass has a record for breaking and entering."

"That's where I know him from. I busted him a few years ago for a break-in at one of the antique stores downtown," Donnelly said.

"Do you really think if he stole the coin, he would have reported to me about Giles coming into his pawn shop?" Gloria asked.

"Maybe he was trying to deflect us away from him," Hank suggested.

"I'm not sure he's smart enough for that, but anything is possible, I guess," Donnelly said.

"Great, now we have a fifth suspect," Nathan said, frustrated with it all. "Look, it's getting late. Let's all head home and take another crack at it tomorrow. Hopefully, Mallory will have a match back on that print tomorrow."

Everyone agreed and got up to leave. Nathan put the Blanton file back in his desk and locked his office door as he went out.

When he got home, he suddenly felt exhausted. It had been a long stressful day, and it was finally hitting him. Just as he sat down on the couch, his cell phone rang. He looked at the caller ID and smiled. "Katherine, how are you?"

"I'm fine. How is everything with you?"

"Good. Is Simon okay?" he asked.

"He's fine. I just gave him his bath, and put him to bed. I emailed you some new photos of him earlier today. Did you get them?"

"Honestly, I didn't have time to check my email today. I was in Boston working on an investigation all day, and just got home. I'll check them later. It will be the perfect thing for me to see before I go to sleep tonight."

"Do you think you'll be coming for a visit soon? He should see his father as often as possible," she asked.

"There's no way I can get away until I get this murder

solved, and the way things are going, it may take a while."

"Okay. Just try to come soon."

He could hear disappointment in her voice. "I'll do my best."

"Take care, Nathan. Bye." She hung up.

Nathan picked up his laptop, and went to the bedroom. He got in bed, opened his personal email, and saw he had received her email. He opened the photos, and saw the smiling face of Simon. Well, smiling as much as a two-month-old child can. His eyelids slowly started falling, and he was soon asleep.

After a good night's sleep, Nathan was ready to start back on the case. There's nothing more he wanted to do than get it solved, so he could take some time off to go see his son.

At his office the next day, Robin called, somewhat frantic. "Nathan, I just discovered something, and you have to hear it."

"What is it?"

"I just found out that Sarah Blanton is selling all of her husband's coins through Alistair's Auction House."

"What about the Doubloon?" he asked.

"I haven't seen the catalog yet, but it looks like she's after money from the coins. The auction is in a couple weeks, but Alistair already has the coins so he can appraise them."

"That is big. Have you talked to him?"

"No, I thought that was something you'd need to do first, especially since Mrs. Blanton works there."

"Thanks for the tip. I definitely want to follow up with him. Oh, don't forget to send me the copy of that life insurance policy."

"I already forgot. I'll get right on that." Just as Robin hung up the call, Mallory popped her head into Nathan's office.

"Got a minute?" she asked.

"Of course. Come in."

"I just wanted to let you know that the State Police got back to me about the fingerprint on Blanton's work phone.

They couldn't find a match."

"That means the print doesn't belong to Bruce Gates. His prints would be on file, since he's an attorney. Do we have Sarah Blanton's prints to compare to?"

"No. I already checked for that," Mallory said.

"Did she ever come to pick up that one coin she brought to us? I called her and told her she could pick it up."

"No. I still have it."

"Well, I think we need to call Mrs. Blanton and tell her she needs to come down here to get it," Nathan said. "Maybe we can get her to hold something in her hand so we can get her prints."

"Can we legally do that?" Mallory asked.

"You bet we can. Thanks for letting me know. I'll give her a call today and see when she can come down here. I'll let you know, then we'll figure out how to get her prints."

He suddenly remembered that he needed to pick up the items from yesterday at Joe Cassidy's office. He wanted to get that done right away, so he headed out the door. He parked in front of Joe's office and walked in.

Joe came out from his private office. "Hi Nathan."

"I need those documents that you used yesterday," Nathan said, getting right to it.

"Sure. I've got them in my office. Come on back."

Nathan followed Joe.

"I didn't want to leave them up front because, well, like you said, they weren't for public view."

Nathan took the items. "Thanks, Joe." He started to leave.

"So, what did I miss yesterday after I left?"

Nathan stopped. "Nothing really, just police business." He again started to leave.

"Oh, one more thing." He pulled a sheet of paper out of his desk, handing it to Nathan.

"What's this?"

"It's my expense report for what I did yesterday. You

know, for mileage, meals, stuff like that. I was going to get paid, wasn't I?"

"All I can do is turn the claim in for you, Joe." This time, he made it outside without being stopped again.

Back at his office, he looked up the phone number for Alistair's Auction House. He needed to talk to Mrs. Blanton, and figured she was back at work.

"Alistair's Auction House."

"Hello. This is Nathan Perry from the Mystic Police Department. Could I speak to Sarah Blanton?"

"One moment." He listened to the music being played on the line while he waited.

"Detective Perry, what can I do for you?" Mrs. Blanton said.

"I just found out that you haven't picked up that coin from our department yet. Since it isn't needed in your husband's case, we really need to get it out of our evidence locker. When can you come pick it up? The sooner, the better."

"Didn't you tell me that coin was valued at a couple hundred dollars?"

"Yes, something like that." He believed she was seeing more dollar signs for her auction.

"Could I come this afternoon?" she asked.

"Yes, that would be fine. What time do you think you'll be here? I want to make sure our evidence clerk will be here to get it for you."

She let out a deep breath. "How about three o'clock?"

"That should be fine. I'll see you then." Nathan hung up the phone, and hurried to Mallory's office. "Sarah Blanton will be here at three. Here's what I want to do."

A little after three, Gloria called Nathan. "Mrs. Blanton is in the lobby waiting to get her coin from evidence. Shall I take her there?"

"No. I'll come get her. Thanks." He walked to the lobby. "Mrs. Blanton, if you'll come with me, I'll take you to get your coin."

She followed him until they reached Mallory's cage. "Mallory, this is Mrs. Blanton," Nathan said. "She's here to pick up that coin that we no longer need."

Mallory stood up and brought a computer tablet to the door of the cage. "You'll need to fill out an online form before I can release the coin to you."

"You have got to be kidding me." She looked at Nathan.

"I have no control over the evidence once it's been logged in. If she says she needs the form filled out, you'll have to do it."

"Good grief." Mrs. Blanton turned the computer around, and started typing. When she finished, she turned it back toward Mallory.

"Thank you. I'll need to print this out for you, and then I'll see if I can find the coin."

"What? You mean you don't have it ready for me to pick up?"

"I can't remove it from it's container until you were here to get it," Mallory said.

"There are no chairs to sit here. Why don't you come back to my office with me while we wait for the coin?" Nathan suggested.

"Very well."

Nathan took her to his office, where they both sat down. "I was glad to find out you had returned to work. It must be difficult to come home to an empty house now."

"No more than usual. I always got home before Chuck."

"I've really developed an interest in coins since working on this case. It's terrible that it took such a tragedy to spur that interest."

"I suppose. Will she take much longer?" Mrs. Blanton asked.

Nathan's cell phone vibrated, indicating a text message. He looked at it, and then put it back on his desk. "Mrs. Blanton, why did you lie to me about having Chuck's work phone?"

"What?" She sat straight up.

"And, why did you delete the two photos of the Doubloon from that phone?"

"You must be crazy." She got up to leave.

"Sit down. I'm not finished." He stood.

She stopped, but did not sit down, so Nathan moved between her and the door. "I picked up the phone from your husband's employer yesterday, and he said you were the one that dropped it off. I also know that two pictures of the Doubloon were deleted from the phone."

"That doesn't mean that I did it."

"No, but we found a fingerprint on the inside of the flip phone. Mallory just compared the fingerprints from the tablet you used to get the coin, and it was a match with the print from the phone. Anything else you want to say?"

"Am I being arrested for something?"

"Not at this time."

"Then, I'm not saying anything without my attorney present," she said.

"If I were you, I'd be getting an attorney, and I don't mean Bruce Gates."

Mallory walked in. "Here is your coin."

Mrs. Blanton grabbed the plastic bag, and stormed out of the office.

"She did not look happy."

"She wasn't. How close of a match do we have on her prints?" Nathan asked.

"They're a perfect match, but I'm going to send them to the MSP to make it official."

"Thanks. Let me know when you get the final results."

Nathan concentrated back on the case at hand. He was still puzzled about James Bass being at the coin shop. He picked up the phone and called him.

"Witch City Pawn Shop. James speaking."

"Mr. Bass, this is Detective Perry from the police department. I was the one that viewed the video from your store."

"Yes, I remember you. What can I do for you, Detective?"

"I was hoping that you could come to the department? I have a few more things I need to ask you."

"Ookkaayy," he said slowly. "When do you need me to come in?"

Nathan looked at his watch. It was getting late. "Could you possibly come in tomorrow morning?"

"Depends on what time. I have to make sure the shop is open, and I don't have any employees."

"What time do you normally open?"

"Nine o'clock."

If you can be here at eight-thirty, I'll be as quick as possible, so you can open on time," Nathan said.

"Well, I guess so."

"Good, I'll see you then." Nathan was done with work for the day, and glad of it. He headed home.

The next morning, he got to work early, just in case Bass came in before eight-thirty. He had picked up a cinnamon roll and his usual coffee from the *Witch's Brew Café* on his way in. He now sat at his desk looking through the morning newspaper.

Gloria buzzed him on the phone a little before eight-thirty. "James Bass is here to see you."

"Thanks. Could you send him back? I'll be at my door watching for him." Nathan got up and stepped to his door. In a few seconds, he saw Bass coming down the hall toward him."

"Thanks for coming in," he said, when Bass reached him. "Come in and sit down." Nathan closed his office door behind them.

"I was kind of surprised to hear from you," Bass said, after sitting down.

"We had something come up that I wanted to speak to you about."

"Sure, anything to help."

"Were you at Bean City Coins several days ago, inquiring

about selling a Doubloon?" Nathan asked.

Bass didn't say anything.

"Before you think about lying." Nathan slapped the photo of him at the shop down on the desk. "Now, let me rephrase my question. Why were you there asking about selling a Doubloon?"

"After you were at my shop asking about that coin, I got curious about how much one of those coins was really worth. That's all. I was just curious."

He seemed rattled, and was acting pretty nervous. "What else do you know that you aren't telling me?"

Bass wet his lips with his tongue. "That guy, you know, the one that was in my shop. I know him."

"You knew him, and didn't tell us? Why the hell didn't you say anything?"

"I was scared. If Will did that guy in, I didn't want him coming after me next," Bass said.

"Do you know where Giles is now, or how to get in touch with him?"

"No sir, I don't, and that's the truth."

"All right. You can go, but you better not be taking any out-of-town trips."

"No sir. I won't." Bass jumped out of his seat, and was out of the office much quicker than when he arrived.

Nathan slept in on Saturday morning. It was around nine-thirty when he started a pot of coffee, and put some bread in the toaster. He heard a key turn in the kitchen door and Ginger walked in to clean the house. "Good morning, Ginger."

"Morning, stud," she replied, putting her coat on the dinette chair. She handed him the newspaper. "I got this out of the box for you."

"What, you didn't bring me breakfast this morning?" he joked with her.

"It's a little late for breakfast, isn't it?" Just then, the toast popped up. She looked at the toaster. "I stand corrected."

Nathan buttered his toast and poured himself some

coffee. "I actually just got up. It's been a long week. I needed the sleep."

Ginger got the broom and dustpan out of the closet and started sweeping. "How is your investigation going?"

"Not nearly as well, as I hoped." A knock came from his front door.

"If you're expecting someone, you should have told me."

"I'm not expecting anyone." He put his toast down, and went to the door.

"Hi, Nathan. I hope I'm not interrupting anything." Dana stood there with coffee in one hand, and a little white bag in the other. "I brought doughnuts."

He opened the door wider to let her in. "There's more coffee in the kitchen, if you need some."

They walked into the kitchen. "Ginger, I didn't know you'd be here," Dana said.

"Ditto." She had put the broom away and was wiping down the counter with a damp cloth. She looked at Nathan. If you're finished in the bedroom, I'll go clean it."

"Go right ahead," he replied.

Ginger left the kitchen, and Dana took a seat at the table. Nathan got his coffee and some napkins, and joined her. She got the doughnuts out.

"I got a call from Paul Hobbs last night. He told me that Blanton's coin collection was being auctioned off as part of his estate in a few weeks," Dana said.

"Why did he call you instead of me?"

"I don't know, but aren't you interested in that bit of news?"

"Yes, it's pertinent to the case."

"That's what I thought. Where's your computer? I want to show you something," she asked.

Nathan went to the bedroom, and brought his laptop back out for her. She set it in front of her and started typing. "Here, look." She turned the computer toward him.

On the screen was the web page for Alistair's Auction

House with photos of several of Blanton's coins on it. "Is the Doubloon listed?" Nathan asked.

"No."

"Did you know Mrs. Blanton works at this auction house?"

"No, I didn't. Now that's interesting," she replied.

Nathan grabbed his cell phone from the counter and dialed a number, putting it on speaker so Dana could hear also.

"Alistair's Auction House, can I help you?"

"This is Detective Perry from the Mystic Police Department. Is Mr. Harris there, by some chance?"

"Yes, if you'll hold, I'll connect you."

After a wait of a few seconds, "This is Alistair Harris."

"Mr. Harris, this is Detective Perry. I'm glad you were in today."

"We have an auction later this afternoon, and I'm always here on auction day. What can I do for you?"

"It's been brought to my attention that Sarah Blanton is selling her husband's coin collection, and I was wondering if she included the Brasher Doubloon?"

"No, it's not included, at least, not yet. Has it been found?" he asked.

"Not to my knowledge."

"We actually have only gone through half of the coins so far. I'm currently having them appraised, and she will bring the other half in to me in a few days."

"Do you know why she's decided to sell them now?"

"She's liquidating everything."

"What do you mean everything?" Nathan asked.

"She's selling her home and moving."

"What? When? Where to?"

"She gave me her two-weeks resignation notice yesterday, and said she was moving to the Adirondack's. I'm not sure when."

"Thank you, Mr. Harris. She wouldn't be working today,

would she?"

"No, she won't be back until Monday."

Nathan ended the call. "Can you believe that? We haven't found her husband's murderer yet, and she's already moving."

"I'm sure she can't pay all the bills at her home with only her job at the auction house," Dana said.

"And, you think she can afford living in the Adirondack Mountains?"

"No, I don't suppose so."

Ginger walked into the kitchen to get the dust mop, and then headed into the living room to clean there.

"Would you like to go to a movie this afternoon? I need to get my mind on something else," he asked.

"I actually can't. I already have plans. Maybe another time."

"You have a date with Joe, right?"

She smiled. "Yes."

"That's okay. I'll find something to do."

"I probably should get going," she said. "Keep me updated, if you find out anything else."

"I will."

Dana left through the living room, and out the front door. Ginger walked back in. "You're a regular playboy, aren't you?" she said.

"What are you talking about? She's going out with someone else now. You saw him at the café the other day."

"I saw him."

"Well, I'm finished for today. Make sure all of your laundry is in the basket and I'll be back Monday morning to do that." Ginger put all of her supplies away and left.

Nathan was studying the case file at his desk on Monday afternoon when his cell phone rang. It showed an unknown number.

"Hello," he answered.

A mousey voice on the other end replied, "I got a

message at the Harrison Street Shelter to call this number."

Nathan realized who it was. "Is this William Giles?"

"Yeah, who's this?"

"Mr. Giles, I'm Nathan Perry with the Mystic Police Department. Please don't hang up."

"What do you want?"

"I need to speak to you about Chuck Blanton."

"Who? I don't know anybody by that name."

"Mr. Blanton was the collector that was killed at the coin convention in Mystic. You were seen talking to him, and I'd like to speak to you about what you may have seen," Nathan said.

"Okay. Ask me now."

"No. I need to speak to you in person. Can you come to the Mystic Police Department?"

"I don't have a car, and no money to pay for a trip to Mystic."

"What if I met you at one of the police precincts in Boston?" Nathan asked.

"I don't really like police departments."

Nathan let out a deep breath. "Where would you like to meet me, Mr. Giles?"

"Maybe at someplace where they have food. I could always use a hot meal," Giles suggested.

"I don't know where would be convenient for you. Name a place."

"There's a cafeteria about three or four blocks from the Harrison Street Shelter. How about we meet there?"

"I can be there by noon," Nathan said.

"I'll meet you out front. Don't bring anyone else with you, especially more cops."

"I understand. I'll see you then."

Giles hung up first. Nathan started gathering the files he would need to take with him for the meeting.

Arriving in Boston, he was able to park near the cafeteria. As he walked closer to the business, he didn't see anyone out front that looked like Giles. He walked up to the door and looked in.

He didn't see him.

He looked up and down the street, and he was beginning to think this was a wasted trip. Then, he looked across the street and saw a man sitting on a rock wall, smoking a cigarette.

It was Giles.

Nathan crossed the street.

The man had a several days' growth of beard and long hair like the photo that Nathan had of him. "William Giles?"

"Yeah."

"I'm Nathan Perry from the Mystic Police Department. What are you doing over here?"

"The cafeteria doesn't like it when homeless people hang around out front of their place."

"I'm hungry. Let's go in," Nathan said.

"You're really going to take me in there to eat?"

"Yes, I am. Come on."

The two men crossed the street and entered the cafeteria. A few of the workers stared at Giles inside, but no one said anything to him. He and Nathan selected their food, and after Nathan paid, they took their trays to a table and sat down.

Nathan could tell Giles was hungry by how quickly he ate the fried chicken on his plate. "You're going to make yourself sick eating so fast."

"I haven't eaten all weekend. If you don't get to the shelters early, you don't eat. They run out of food. I picked the busiest shelters over the weekend, and didn't get any food," Giles explained.

Nathan felt sorry for him. He'd had some bad food while in Afghanistan, but he never went without. "If you're still hungry after you finish, I can get you more, if you want."

Giles finished the last bite of his cherry pie, and said he was full. "You said you had some questions for me."

"It's nice weather out today. How about we walk down

the street to that park and talk there?" Nathan suggested.

Giles agreed. On the way to the park, Nathan stopped to get them both some coffee from a street vendor. They entered the park, and Nathan chose a bench away from what few people were in there that day.

He took out the photo of Giles talking to Blanton and showed it to him. "Do you remember talking to Blanton at the convention?"

"Yeah, kinda."

"What were you doing at the coin convention?" Nathan asked.

"A friend was going to Mystic, and I thought it would be a nice change of scenery. I was wrong."

"Why were you wrong about that?"

"Mystic is for people with money. There's no shelters or soup kitchens."

"You're right about no shelters, but there are places you can go for food. You just didn't know where they were."

"Surveillance video from the bar in the hotel showed you sitting in the bar when Blanton was in there. What do you remember about being in the bar?"

"Not much was going on in there. I went in there hoping to get some free drinks. I got one. Was this guy the one that was getting loud in there?" Giles asked.

"Yes."

"I didn't really understand what he was talking about, but he was saying something about some valuable coin he had."

"You were seen leaving right after he did. Where did you go?"

Giles stood up. "What's going on here? Do you think I killed that guy?"

"Calm down. I didn't come here with any intention of arresting you for anything. I just need to know what you saw that night." He was mostly telling Giles the truth. He sat back down, but Nathan noticed he was tense, and looked like he was ready to bolt at any minute. He then showed Giles the other photo he had. "Is this you at the Witch City Pawn Shop the next day in Mystic?"

Giles looked at the photo. "Yeah, that's me."

"What were you doing in there?"

"I asked the guy if he bought watches. He said he had too many already. Then I asked him where a guy could stay at night in town, and not get arrested."

"Where did he say to go?"

"He said he didn't know, but there were lots of nice parks around town."

"You didn't go back to Boston?"

"My friend left town without me. I ended up sleeping in Chapin Park. I think that's what the sign said."

"You didn't ask him about buying any coins?" Nathan asked.

"Coins? No, just an old watch I had. I thought maybe I could get enough money to get a ticket for the ferry to Boston."

"If I need to get ahold of you again, how can I do that?"

"Leave me a message at the Harrison Street Shelter. I'll get it."

Nathan gave him his card. "If you think of anything about that night, call me."

Giles took the card, and started to walk away, but stopped and turned back to Nathan. "Thanks for the meal." Then, he left.

Nathan sat on the bench for a few minutes before two men approached him. It was Hank with Ryan Avery, who had been watching from a distance.

"You let him go?" Hank asked.

"There wasn't anything to hold him on," Nathan said. "He's still a suspect though."

Chapter Ten

When Nathan got to his office on Tuesday morning, he could hear his phone ringing inside. He quickly unlocked the door and grabbed the phone. "Hello."

"Good morning. I thought I was going to have to call your cell phone," Robin said.

"I stopped for breakfast this morning."

"I have news."

Nathan sat down behind his desk. "What's that?" He took off his coat as he listened.

"The name of the life insurance salesman is Roscoe Mullins."

"Is he the source you wouldn't tell me about?"

"No."

"How long have you known his name?"

"A little while. I wanted to try to talk to him first."

"How did that go?" Nathan took a drink of his coffee.

There was a short pause. "He wouldn't talk to me."

"So, you figured he would talk to me since I'm a police officer? He's probably lawyered up already, that is if he hasn't left the country."

"I'm sorry, but my story has to come first."

"No, catching a murderer has to come first." He let out a deep breath. "Thanks for the information. I'll check on his background and see what I can find out. If I can still find him,

I'll talk to him. Please don't contact him again."

"Glad I could help," she replied sarcastically, and hung up.

He knew that didn't go well, but he was getting a little tired of her deciding what information to tell him and when.

"Good morning, Nathan." Gloria stood at his doorway, coffee cup in hand. "How are you this morning?"

"Not bad, I guess."

"You look like your world is falling apart. What's up?" She stepped into his office and sat down.

"I just found out the name of the insurance salesman that wrote Blanton's big policy."

"That sounds good."

"Getting that information probably cost me my relationship with Robin."

"That's too bad, but-" she stopped mid-sentence.

"But, what?"

She paused before continuing. "Well, I never thought you two made a good match."

"You never saw us together."

"Let me ask you this, do you really like her, or were you together because she was investigating the murder for her articles?"

Nathan thought for a minute. Could Gloria be right? Could he have wanted that relationship because of her connection to the case. "She did promise to take me to a Patriots game with seats in her magazine's suite." He laughed, and Gloria did too.

"What's your next step, now that you have the insurance guy's name?" she asked.

"I was just getting ready to run his name through the DMV database." He started typing, and Gloria moved behind him to watch. "Hmmm, nothing more than a couple minor speeding violations." He hit print. At least he had his home address. Next, he checked Mullins' criminal record. It was clean. "I didn't think I'd find anything since he's a licensed insurance salesman."

"What about his financial record, or his connections?" Gloria asked.

"I definitely want to check his financials, but I'll have to get a warrant for that. I don't have a clue how to find out who his connections are since his criminal record is clean."

"What about checking social media?" she suggested.

"How do I do that?"

"I can do it," she offered.

"You go right ahead. That would be a big help."

"I'll let you know what I find," she said, and left.

While Gloria went to work on the social media idea, Nathan started on the paperwork to get a warrant for Mullins' financial records. Finished, he printed the document, and then walked it over to Judge Mason's office at the courthouse.

Nathan entered the judge's office. "Good morning, Detective Perry," the secretary said.

"Good morning. Is the judge available? I have a warrant request."

"He should be." She picked up the phone and pushed two buttons. " Detective Perry is here to see you about a warrant." She listened and then hung up the phone. "You can go in."

He entered the judge's office, finding him sitting at this desk. "Good morning, your Honor."

"Sit down, Perry. What's this warrant for?"

Nathan handed him the paperwork. The judge put his glasses on, looking over the document.

"How many warrants have you requested on this case?" Judge Mason asked.

"I don't know the exact number, but it's been several."

"Have you made any progress on this case so far with these warrants? Ruled anyone out, or found evidence that will lead to an arrest?"

"Well, not yet, sir."

"I don't like it when officers try to take advantage of the

of the court system by making requests on hunches, and then not getting results."

"I understand, sir. My requests weren't made on hunches. There are several suspects in this case. I know the number of warrants has been excessive, but each one has been crucial for the investigation," Nathan explained.

Judge Mason looked over the document again. "I'm going to approve this one." He signed the document and handed it back to Nathan. "I hope you can get some solid results from it. It won't be easy getting another one from me."

"Thank you, sir. I'll do my best." Nathan left and went back to the police department.

When he walked into the lobby of the department, Gloria motioned for him. He pulled a chair up behind her. "What's up?"

"Here's what I found on socia media about Mullins."

Nathan looked at the papers she gave him. "You did all this in such a short time?"

"Yes. It was easy."

"Thank you." Nathan took the printed pages to his office. He sat down at his desk and started reading. Gloria had done an extensive search.

Hank stepped into Nathan's office. "Gloria said I should ask you about her research."

"Sit down." He handed some of the pages to him. "She did one of the best background checks I've seen. I'm going to go question him this afternoon."

"Need any help on that?"

"What I need is if you could take this warrant and get his financial information before I go."

"I can do that." Hank took the warrant and left the office to get busy on it.

Nathan went back to reading the background check. He had only gone through about half of it when he decided he needed a break. It was close to noon, so he called Ginger's café to put an order in for a take-out lunch. By the time he walked down there, it should be ready.

The Witch's Brew had its usual lunch crowd. Since he had been in Mystic for a while now, everyone seemed to know him, and they all greeted him as he walked to the counter.

"Just a take-out lunch today?" Ginger asked, taking his money.

"It's a busy day. No time for a sit-down lunch today. I'll be eating at my desk." He took the foam container, and walked back to the department. Gloria jumped up from her post as soon as he walked in.

"I have to tell you something. Let's go to your office." She practically pulled him along to his office. Once inside, she closed the door. "You aren't going to believe what I found."

Nathan put his food on his desk and sat down. "What did you find?"

She shoved a sheet of paper into his face.

"What's this?"

"It's Mullins' family tree from an online genealogy site. Look at who his brother is," she said.

Nathan looked at the paper, but it was confusing to him.

"Here. Look here." She pointed to a specific place on the paper.

"Well, I'll be damn," Nathan said. "This could be the link we've been looking for. Excellent job, Gloria."

"Thank you. I was on my break, and one of those DNA test kit commercials came on the television. That gave me the idea to check the genealogy sites to see if I could find out who he was related to."

"As soon as I eat my lunch, I'm going to head to his company's office and pick him up for questioning at the State Police building. I don't know if I'll be back today, but you can reach me by my cell phone, if you need me for anything."

"Good luck."

While he ate lunch, he wrote down a list of questions to ask Mullins.

Hank walked into the office. "Here you go. This guy is

deep in debt, and doesn't have a lot of money on hand." He handed him several pages of a printout.

Nathan wiped his hands on a napkin before taking the pages. "This is good. Thanks. Look what Gloria dug up." He handed Hank the Mullins family tree.

"This is huge."

"I know. I'm going to go talk to Mullins today."

"I wish I could go with you, but we had a couple guys call in sick today, so we're short staffed."

"I understand. I'll talk to you when I get back."

Hank left for his patrol. Nathan took his food container to the breakroom to toss in the trash. Back in his office, he put everything he would need for the questioning in his leather portfolio. He called Gloria to tell her he was leaving to interview Mullins, got his coat, and hit the road for Boston.

Thanks to light traffic, forty-five minutes later, Nathan entered Boston's city limits. The Boston Life Insurance Company office was on the west side of town. He parked his car in a parking lot, and entered the building.

"Welcome to Boston Life. How can I help you?" the young lady behind the counter said.

She was a little too cheerful for Nathan after his drive from Mystic. "I need to see Roscoe Mullins."

"Certainly. Is this about a policy?"

"You could say that."

"Your name?"

"Nathan Perry," he replied.

"Thank you. If you'll have a seat, he'll be right with you."

There were only about ten other people in the lobby. Nathan sat away from most of them.

After waiting about ten minutes, the lobby door opened. "Nathan Perry."

Nathan stood and walked up to the man, who held his hand out. "Roscoe Mullins." They shook hands. "I understand you need to see me about a policy? Right this way."

"Thank you," Nathan said.

They walked down a long hallway, with Mullins' office being about halfway back. "Here we are. Please, sit down." The two men sat. "Did someone refer you to me?" Mullins asked.

"Yes, in a manner of speaking. Bruce Gates."

"Bruce? How do you know Bruce?"

Nathan took his badge out to show to Mullins. "I'm with the Mystic Police Department investigating the murder of Chuck Blanton."

The color left Mullins' face when he saw the badge. "I don't know anything about that," he said.

"We know that you issued a life insurance policy on Chuck for half-a-million dollars, and that Chuck's signature was forged on the policy. Do you have anything to say about that?"

"I-I-I, no. I have nothing to say," he responded.

Nathan stood and took out his handcuffs. "That's probably wise. Roscoe Mullins, you're under arrest for insurance fraud, and possibly accessory to murder. Stand up." He handcuffed him behind his back and marched him out.

At the doorway to the lobby, the ladies behind the counter gasped when they saw them. Nathan held up his badge.

"Sherry, call my attorney, Bruce Gates. He's in the book. I'll be at the Mystic Police Department," Mullins said, as they walked out.

Nathan put Mullins in the back seat of his unmarked car, and then got into the driver's seat. On the highway, Nathan passed the exit to Mystic, instead turning toward downtown.

"Hey, you missed the exit. Where are we going?" Mullins asked.

"I'm taking you to the State Police building for questioning." He picked up his cell phone and called Sam Denzinger. "Sam, it's Nathan. I have a suspect I need to question. Could I bring him to your building and use a room?"

"Sure, Nathan. When will you be here?" Denzinger

asked.

"In about ten minutes, depending on traffic."

"I'll meet you in the lobby."

Nathan ended the call. When he pulled into the parking lot he parked the car next to the building in a designated spot for visiting police officers. He got Mullins out and escorted him into the lobby where Denzinger was waiting for them.

"Thanks for letting me use a room," Nathan said.

"Anytime. Come with me." Denzinger took them to an interogation room.

Nathan removed Mullins' handcuffs. "Sit down." He turned to Denzinger. "You want to stay?"

"If you don't mind," he replied.

Nathan sat down at the table across from Mullins. Denzinger leaned against the wall near the door.

Before Nathan began the questioning, he read Mullins his rights. "Do you understand these rights as I have read them?"

"Yes," Mullins replied. "I'd like to wait for Bruce to be here."

"I have a feeling Mr. Gates won't be showing up, even if he knew I brought you here instead of Mystic. He has his own problems," Nathan said. "The State Police handwriting expert has determined that the signature on the life insurance police was not Chuck Blanton's. Who signed the policy?"

"Can I please call an attorney?" Mullins requested.

"Sure. Who do you want to call?" Nathan asked.

"I don't know. I don't think I can afford one."

Nathan looked over at Denzinger, who picked up the phone on the wall. "We need a public defender in Interrogation Room One." He waited for an answer. "Thanks." He hung up the phone. "Someone will be here in about fifteen minutes."

Nathan nodded, and turned back to Mullins. "Who signed the policy?"

"You can't ask me any questions until my attorney gets here."

"No, you're wrong about that. I can ask all the questions I want, but you don't have to answer them until an attorney is present," Nathan said.

"Well, I'm not going to answer anything until he gets here."

"That is your right. We've got you for insurance fraud, and that alone means you'll lose your insurance license, ending your income. You'll also probably serve a little time, and be on probation for even longer than that. If we tack on the accessory to murder, your kids will be out of high school, and maybe even out of college, by then."

"I didn't have anything to do with the murder."

"You're in a lot of debt, Roscoe. You needed money. How much were you going to get out of the insurance payout?"

Mullins didn't say anything.

"We know Blanton's wife and Bruce Gates are involved in the murder, and with her getting the money from the life insurance policy that you wrote up, that pulls you in with them. It's the connection we needed to bring you in. Not to mention, we know Bruce Gates is your brother-in-law."

Mullins eyes widened. Nathan looked at Denzinger, who also showed astonishment. He looked back at Mullins. "Once we arrest Bruce and Sarah, whoever sings first about what happened, will likely get a leaner sentence."

Someone knocked at the door. Denzinger opened it. A man in a trenchcoat walked in. "I'm Richard Alden, public defender for Mr. Mullins."

"I'm Detective Perry from the Mystic Police Department, and this is Detective Denzinger from the State Police."

"Gentlemen," Alden shook their hands. "I'd like to speak to my client alone, please."

Nathan and Denzinger stepped into the hallway, closing the door behind them.

"Bruce Gates is his brother-in-law?" Denzinger asked.

"Yeah, Gloria did a search on a genealogy site and discovered a nice bit of information," Nathan said.

"I would have never thought about doing that."

"Me, either. She's turned into a first-rate police officer. She's going to go far."

"You think the wife and Gates did it then?" Denzinger asked.

"I do. With Mullins' help, I hope I can get a conviction on them."

"His attorney will want a deal."

"I think our district attorney will be happy to cut a deal, if it means a murder conviction."

"You're probably still going to need more than Mullins' statement. Have you checked the state's handgun permit file to see if Blanton or Gates has a gun?"

"I didn't think of that," Nathan said.

"After we finish here, we can go to my office to check."

The door to the interrogation room opened and Alden stepped out. "You can come back in now."

Nathan and Denzinger stepped back into the room and sat down.

"My client says you're going to charge him with insurance fraud, and accessory to murder. Is that correct?" Alden asked.

"It is," Nathan replied.

"Is there some sort of deal we can get for Mr. Mullins, if he cooperates with the murder investigation?"

"Obviously, I can't guarantee anything, since the DA in Mystic is the one to make that decision, but if what he has to say is pertinent to the case, I think a deal can be reached."

"When can we speak to the DA?" Alden asked.

"I need to take Mullins back to Mystic to book him there. If District Attorney Grant is available, I'm sure you can talk to him by the end of the day."

"Let's do that then. Roscoe, I'll meet you in Mystic at the end of the day. Don't say anything to Detective Perry on the drive to Mystic."

"I understand," Mullins replied.

Alden walked out the room with Nathan and Denzinger.

"I'll need to check on something before we leave, but I guess I'll see you later in Mystic," Nathan said.

Alden nodded and left. Denzinger had an officer go into the room with Mullins, while he and Nathan went to his office.

Denzinger sat at his computer and pulled up the database. "What was Gates' first name again?"

"Bruce."

After typing in a few things, the computer popped up with what they needed. "Here it is. Gates does have a license to carry a firearm, which probably means he owns one."

"Would you print that for me?" Nathan asked.

Denzinger hit a button. Almost immediately, the printer spit out the document. Nathan placed it in his folder. "Thanks. If I need anything else, I'll let you know."

He took custody of Mullins. He put him in the backseat of his car, and drove back to Mystic.

Once at the Mystic Police Department, Nathan took Mullins in through the sally port. He was booked, fingerprinted, photographed, and given a set of jail clothes. With Mullins now in custody of corrections, Nathan went to his office before going home for the day. He saw that the voicemail light on his phone was flashing, indicating a message. He sat down and pushed a button on the phone.

"Nathan, this is Daniel Grant. I spoke to Roscoe Mullins' attorney. I think we can get a conviction for the insurance fraud, but we're going to need a little more to get a murder charge filed. Call me in the morning."

How much more could he need to get that murder charge, he thought to himself.

Nathan slept well Thursday night, waking up Friday morning in a good mood, regardless of the news from Daniel Grant. On the way to work, he stopped by the bakery in town to buy several dozen doughnuts for everyone. He put the boxes on a table in the breakroom, grabbing a couple for himself, before getting his coffee and going to his office.

He had just taken his first bite when Daniel Grant appeared

at his door. "Dan, please come in," he mumbled while chewing, and then swallowing. "Would you like a doughnut?"

Grant came in and sat down. "No, thanks. I came in early to meet with Mullins and his attorney, but wanted to speak with you first."

Nathan took a drink of his coffee. "What's up? I got your voicemail last night."

"His attorney said that Mullins will admit that Blanton's wife and Gates wanted Blanton dead for the insurance money, but he has no evidence that they actually did it."

"Gates has a handgun permit. I was just going to check to see if it's registered, to see what he owns." Nathan logged onto his computer and pulled up the Massachusetts Criminal Justice database. He entered Gates' name. "Here it is. He owns a 9mm, same caliber that Blanton was killed with." He printed two copies, giving one to Grant.

"We need that gun to check ballistics. Right now, all I have on Gates is forgery and insurance fraud," Grant said. "After we talk to Mullins, I'll file the fraud charges on him, and start the paperwork on Gates. You'll need to get a warrant to get that gun."

"Oh, no." Nathan leaned on his desk with his head in his hands.

"What's wrong?"

Nathan sat back in his chair. "I got a huge lecture from Judge Mason Tuesday about all the warrants I've requested with no results from them. I can't go to him again for another one."

Grant stood. "Let me take care of getting the warrant."

"That would be great. Thank you."

"I'll get right on that, as soon as I get back to my office."

Nathan's phone rang. "Perry--- Thanks, Gloria." He hung up the phone. "Richard Alden is here. We can question Mullins now."

Grant grabbed Nathan's second doughnut and took a bite. "Let's go."

The Coin Collector

***

Later that afternoon, Nathan had the warrant in hand, and he and Hank were at Bruce Gates' law office to serve it.

"Mr. Gates, we have a warrant for any and all 9mm handguns you have," Nathan said.

"What? You think I killed Chuck. That's ridiculous," Gates said.

"Think what you want. Do you have a 9mm gun here at your office?"

Gates snatched the warrant from Nathan's hand to read. "The only one I have is at my apartment."

"Good. You can ride with us," Nathan said, opening Gates' office door.

At Gates' apartment, he led the officers to the bedroom where he retrieved the handgun from the drawer next to the bed. He unloaded it, and handed it and the ammo to Hank.

"Thank you, Mr. Gates," Hank said, as Gates dropped it into the evidence bag. After sealing the bag, Hank wrote something on it, and then both he and Nathan signed it.

"Is this the only gun you have?" Nathan asked.

"It's my only gun," Gates replied.

"What about Mrs. Blanton? Do you know if she has a gun?" Hank asked.

"You'd have to ask her."

"Thank you for your cooperation Mr. Gates. We'll be in touch," Nathan said. "I don't have to explain to you to stay in town, do I?"

"You don't. I know the routine. I want that gun back after it's cleared," Gates said.

Nathan didn't respond to that, only asked, "Can we give you a ride back to your office?"

"No, thank you. I'll call an Uber."

The two officers left. Gates slammed the door behind them. "Wow, was that sarcasm, or not," Hank said.

Nathan laughed. "He was trying to be a smartass. It

didn't work."

They got into their car, with Hank in the driver's seat. "Where to now?"

"We need to take the gun to the State Police lab for a ballistics check before we head back to Mystic."

Hank put the car into drive and headed for the police lab. "Gates didn't seem to be worried too much about us checking the ballistics of the gun."

"I thought that too."

"Do you think he was just being cocky, or does he really know this isn't the gun that killed Blanton?" Hank asked.

"Let's go see Sarah Blanton before we take the gun to ballistics." Nathan punched her address into the GPS. They turned at the next street.

"Why?"

"I want to see if she will turn over any guns to us," Nathan said.

It took twenty minutes to get to the Blanton home. Sure enough, just as Robin had told him, there was a real estate sign in the front yard. They got out of the car and went to the door. Mrs. Blanton answered after the second knock.

"Detective Perry, I wasn't expecting you," she said.

"Oh, I doubt that. I'm sure Bruce called you as soon as we left his place, am I right?" Nathan asked.

"What if he did? There's no law against that."

"You're right, there isn't. So, I assume you know that we are here to ask if you or Chuck own a gun, and, if so, would you turn that gun over to us?"

"Neither Chuck or I have ever owned a gun." She started to close the door, but Hank stuck his foot out, blocking it.

"We know you and Gates defrauded the life insurance company, and you'll pay for that," Nathan said. "You better get a lawyer, and one that is smarter than your boyfriend." He nodded to Hank, who moved his foot as she slammed the door shut.

"Twice in one day. I believe that's a record for me," Hank

joked.

"Not me."

Their next stop was the State Police lab. Nathan and Hank entered the building, passing through the security gate showing their credentials. The ballistics lab was on the second floor and to the right of the elevator.

"Hi, Phil," Nathan said to the technician through the window.

"Hello, Detective Perry. What can I do for you today?"

Nathan took the gun out of his briefcase, and placed it into the drawer under the window. "I need to have this checked against case number two, eight, five, three."

The technician pulled the drawer in and took the bag out. He filled out a card and put it in the drawer for Nathan to sign, and then pulled it back in. "Thanks, Detective Perry. I'll get this in the rotation. We should have the results back to you next week."

"Thanks, Phil." Nathan and Hank left the building, and started their drive back to Mystic.

"If Gates' gun isn't a match, what's our next move?" Hank asked.

"I'm not sure. We can still arrest Gates and Mrs. Blanton on insurance fraud, and maybe conspiracy to murder, but that's about it, since Mullins couldn't produce the evidence we need."

Chapter Eleven

When Nathan got to work on Monday morning, he had an idea. On a whim, he googled, Brasher Doubloon. He couldn't believe what he found. A Brasher Doubloon was scheduled to be auctioned off next month at the Williams Auction House in Providence, Rhode Island. This could be the break he needed in this case. He jotted down the phone number and called them.

"Williams Auction House."

"Hello. My name is Nathan Perry. I'm a detective with the Mystic, Massachusetts Police Department, and I need to speak to someone about the Brasher Doubloon coin that is listed for auction on your web site."

"One moment, I'll connect you with our Auction Director."

Nathan waited while listening to the classical music that played over the phone.

"Detective Perry?" a female voice came over the line.

"Yes."

"This is Lauren Kingsbury. I'm the Auction Director. How can I help you with the coin?"

"I'm working on a case where a Brasher Doubloon was stolen. I'm sure you know how rare these coins are, and I was hoping you could give me the name of the person who currently owns the coin you're auctioning."

"Detective, I'm sure you know that we, as most other auction houses, promise anomimity to the owners of the items we auction. I'm sorry, I can't release the name," she said.

With the lecture he got from the judge, he didn't dare ask for another warrant until he had tried everything to get the information. "Miss Kingsbury, it is Miss, isn't it?"

"Yes, but that will not make any difference in my decision to give you the name you want."

"I didn't want to say this at first, but this is actually a murder case. A coin collector was murdered over this coin."

"Really?"

He was pretty sure her response was sarcasm.

"Why didn't you just say that in the first place?"

"I didn't want to shock you with the violent crime that the coin caused." Even he didn't believe that.

"I'm sorry, Detective."

"You realize I'll get a warrant."

"I do, and I also know that you're in another state, and it'll take quite a while to get."

"You'll be hearing from me sooner than you think." He hung up the call.

Hank stuck his head in Nathan's doorway. "Got a minute?"

"Sure. Come on in."

He took a seat in front of Nathan's desk. "How was your weekend?"

"Not bad. My sister came down Saturday. She spent the whole day pointing out to me what needed to be fixed at the house, as if I didn't know."

"I thought you owned the house."

"Her name is still on it too, until I can buy out her half."

"Did you spend Sunday fixing everything?"

"No. I watched football all day." Both men laughed.

"How's the murder case coming? Anything new?"

"As a matter of fact, yes. I had a break in the case, and then hit a brick wall." Nathan took a drink of his coffee. He spun his laptop around and showed him the screen with the Doubloon on the auction house web site.

"That has to be our coin, right?"

"I hope so. I just got off the phone with the auction house. They won't cooperate without a warrant."

"What's the problem? Just have Judge Mason sign a warrant," Hank said.

Nathan filled him in on his lecture from the judge last week.

Hank looked closer at the computer screen. "The auction house is in Rhode Island. What if you got a warrant signed by a judge there?"

"Do you know a judge in Rhode Island?" Nathan asked.

"Not me personally, but we both know someone who knows people there that can probably get it for us."

"Who?"

"Chief Cabot is originally from Providence. I think he even started his police career there. He probably knows someone who can get the warrant for you."

"I guess that's my only choice. I hate like hell to tell him that Judge Mason is pissed at all the warrants I've requested that turned nothing up."

Hank stood. "If there's anything I can help you with, let me know."

"Since you mentioned that."

"I was so close," Hank joked.

"Could you get the financial information on Roscoe Mullins for me? I have a feeling I'll be driving to Rhode Island today."

"Sure. I've become the expert in getting financials." Hank took the warrant that Nathan held out to him, and left the office.

Nathan picked up the phone and called the chief. "Chief, this is Perry. If you aren't too busy, I'd like to come up and update you on the Blanton murder case."

The chief told him to come up. He stepped off the elevator

and around the corner to Chief Cabot's office. However, he stopped dead in his tracks when he got to the open doorway. "I'm sorry, chief. I didn't know Mayor Cranston was with you. I can come back later."

"Nonsense, Detective," the mayor said. "Come in. I want to hear the update also."

Nathan took a seat next to the mayor. "Well, Perry, go ahead," the chief said.

"Yes, sir. We finally found out who sold Mr. Blanton the big life insurance policy and made the arrest for insurance fraud, with more charges pending. I probably should also tell you that when I went to see Judge Mason last week, he wasn't too happy about issuing another warrant without the previous ones producing any usable information."

"That's just great, Perry. Nothing like pissing off the judge," the chief said.

The mayor looked at Chief Cabot.

"Appologies for my language, ma'am," he said. He looked back at Nathan. "What else?"

"I discovered today that a coin like the one that is missing from the murder scene is being sold next month at an auction house in Providence, Rhode Island. Since I'm on thin ice with Judge Mason, I was wondering if you have any contacts in Providence that might help us get a warrant from a judge there?"

The chief pursed his lips, thinking. "I used to work at the police department there many years ago. I know the chief there. Let me give him a call and see what I can do. Email the info you have on the auction house to me."

"Yes, sir." Nathan got up and nodded to the mayor as he left the office. Back in his office, he called the district attorney.

"Daniel Grant's office," his secretary said.

"This is Nathan Perry. Could I speak to Mr. Grant, if he's available?"

"Yes, Detective. One moment."

"Nathan, what can I do for you," Grant almost

immediately answered.

"Thanks for taking my call, Daniel. I need to get a warrant for an auction house in Rhode Island. Could you tell me what I need to do? Chief Cabot said he knows the police chief there and would enlist his help."

"Is this for the Blanton case?" Grant asked.

"Yes, it is. I found out that they're auctioning a Doubloon next month, and want to find out who is selling it. They won't release the info without a warrant."

"If the chief knows someone, it's probably better that they fill out the request for the warrant. I assume you're going to Providence?"

"Yes, probably today."

"Take your case file. They'll need as much information as possible for the request."

"Thanks, Daniel. I'll let you know what I find." They ended the call. Feeling hungry now, he decided to go to Ginger's for lunch.

With it still being a nice day, he decided to walk to the café. He opened the door to go in, and found the place pretty busy for a Tuesday. He didn't see any empty tables, so he took a seat at the counter, and picked up a menu.

"What can I get you today?" Ginger asked.

Nathan lowered the menu. "What's the special today?"

"It's a barbeque chicken sandwich with one side, and the soup is clam chowder."

"I'll take the sandwich with steamed broccoli, and a Coke." He put the menu back in its holder.

Ginger wrote the order down and turned around, handing it to the cook through the window. She brought Nathan his drink, setting it down in front of him. "How's your day going?"

"Not bad. Things seem to finally be falling into place with work today."

Ginger looked past him and went to take care of a customer. Nathan took a drink of his soda. He saw the newspaper laying near him, and picked it up to look through it. Most of the stories had to do with the upcoming elections. There was a story about a police officer and a suspect having a scuffle, with the officer being slightly hurt. He really needed to start going to roll call in the mornings to know what was going on in the department, he thought to himself. The sports section noted the latest win of the Mystic High School football team.

Ginger came back with his food. "I'm still cleaning egg off my front door every morning."

"I'll say something to the shift sergeant again about that," he replied, taking a bite of his sandwich.

Someone sat down next to Nathan at the counter. "Hello, Detective."

He turned to see Paul Hobbs next to him. He wiped his mouth with a napkin. "Hello, Mr. Hobbs. How are you?"

"Fine, fine. Have you caught the murderer yet?"

"No, not yet. Have you heard anything in the coin collecting grapevine?"

"Nothing, other than all the collectors wanting to know who did it?"

Ginger brought a cup of coffee to Hobbs, who ordered the chowder.

"I really appreciate the help you gave me educating me on coin collecting. It's an interesting hobby. I'm thinking of buying my son some coins as an investment for him."

"How old is he?" Hobbs asked.

"He's a newborn, almost two months old now." He took another bite of food.

"You should get a mint set of all the coins from his birth year. Stop by, and see me sometime. I'll show you what to order."

"I'd really appreciate that. Thanks. Would that be a good investment?"

"Well, you won't pay for his college education with it, but it's a good collectable item for him."

"I collected stamps as a kid, but never thought about coins. I guess I figured they'd be too expensive to get."

"If you collect new, uncirculated coins, it can get expensive. Most kids start out collecting coins from their parents' extra change," Hobbs said.

"There's a lot to this hobby, isn't there?"

"It can be."

Nathan motioned for Ginger. "Could I have a large coffee to-go?"

She filled a large to-go cup with coffee and placed a lid on it. "Here you go," she said.

Nathan put some money on the counter. "Thanks, Ginger. I'll be in touch, Mr. Hobbs." Nathan left for his walk back to the office.

Only a few seconds after sitting back down at his desk, his phone rang. "Perry."

"I'm so glad you were in."

"Robin, I didn't think I'd hear from you so soon." He leaned back in his chair.

"I found something today that I thought you might need to know. Sarah Blanton and Bruce Gates applied for a marriage license this morning."

He sat back up. "You're kidding. I sent his gun to the State Police to have the ballistics checked with the bullet that killed Chuck. Maybe he's getting a little nervous and doesn't want Sarah to testify against him."

"Was it a match?" she asked.

"I haven't got the results back yet." He debated in his mind whether to tell her about the Doubloon he found up for auction.

"You will keep me updated, right?"

"Sure." He decided to keep that bit of information to himself for now.

"What are you going to do about the newly engaged couple?"

"I'm not sure. I have something I have to do this

afternoon, and can't get up there to talk to them."

"There's a three-day waiting period before they can get married. That gives you a little time."

"I didn't know that. Maybe I can talk to them tomorrow. Thanks for letting me know about that."

"If you come up to Boston tomorrow, maybe we could get together for lunch or dinner?"

He was tempted, but not sure if it was a good idea. He had felt them drifting apart lately. "I'll have to let you know on that."

"Oh, sure. No problem. Just give me a call."

"I will. Thanks, again." She hung up first. It was an awkward ending for the call. Nathan was pretty sure she understood that neither lunch or dinner would happen.

Gloria stepped into his office holding a pink memo page. "You were gone to lunch and the chief said to give this to you." She handed him the note.

"Thanks." It was the name of the police chief in Providence, and it also said that the chief there would help him with the warrant.

"You're going to Providence?" Gloria asked.

"It looks like I am."

"I don't suppose you need someone to go with you, do you?"

He knew Gloria was anxious to get out and work in the field again. "I really don't think I need anyone else today, but I might need your help if I question Mrs. Blanton again."

"I'll be glad to help."

"There is one thing you can do for me today though."

She perked right up. "What do you need?"

"I've heard that Sarah Blanton and Bruce Gates have applied for a marriage license in Boston. Could you call and get the information on that application. I understand there's a waiting period. Find out for sure when they applied, and anything else on that application."

"I'll get right on that. You have a safe trip today." She

turned, and headed back to her desk up front, humming as she walked away.

Nathan chuckled to himself. Gloria was a fantastic woman. He was happy to have her as a co-worker and friend.

He picked up the phone and called the Providence police chief to make sure he would be in his office. Nathan told him he'd be there in a few hours. Before leaving town, he stopped by his house to pack a bag. Chances were, he'd be spending the night in Providence, and go to the auction house in the morning.

Two hours later, he parked in the parking garage across the street from the police department in Providence, and walked to the building.

"Good afternoon, can I help you?" the lady said from behind the glass window in the lobby.

"I'm Detective Nathan Perry from the Mystic, Massachusetts Police Department. I'm here to see Chief Latham." He held up his badge to the lady.

"Please have a seat. I'll tell him you're here, Detective."

Nathan opted to stand, since he had been sitting so long on the drive there. It only took a few minutes for the chief to appear at the door.

"Detective Perry."

Nathan stepped to the door.

"I'm Martin Latham, Providence police chief."

Nathan shook his hand. "It's nice to meet you. Chief Cabot extends his gratitude for helping me with this."

Latham led Nathan to his office. "Paul and I were partners on the force here a long time ago."

"Interesting how both of you ended up being police chiefs."

"We compare notes all the time. He said you're doing a fine job as detective."

Nathan was shocked to hear that Chief Cabot had said that, but it felt good. "That's nice to hear. He's a good chief to have around."

They reached Chief Latham's office and both sat down. "Now that we have both told each other lies, let's get down to business."

Nathan explained about the murders, the coin, and the suspects. "Yesterday, I discovered that the Williams Auction House in Providence has a Doubloon going up for auction next month. I called them, but they refused to give me any information unless I have a warrant. Hence, why I am here."

"That sounds good enough to me." He opened his laptop. "Move your chair over here, so you can help me get the information correct."

After getting the file out of his leather portfolio, he moved the chair next to the chief. He fed him the information, and the chief typed it onto the computer. It didn't take long before the chief hit print, and the form came out of the printer behind them.

Nathan took it off and looked it over before handing it to Chief Latham. "It looks good to me."

The chief then looked at it. "This should do it. I'll have one of my officers take it over to the judge for his signature, but it will likely be tomorrow before we get it back."

"That's fine. I had planned on spending the night. Can you recommend a hotel?" Nathan asked.

"There's a Best Western not too far from here, and it should fit into your department's budget." The chief gave him directions, and Nathan left to find the hotel.

Around ten the next morning, Nathan walked into the police department. The lady at the front window recognized him right away and buzzed open the door. "He's expecting you," she said.

He headed down the hallway and saw that the door to Chief Latham's office was open. He was on the phone, but waved Nathan into the room.

Once finished with his call, he hung up. "I received your warrant about thirty minutes ago. Would you like an officer to take you?"

"I'd welcome any assistance. I don't really know my way around the city very well."

Chief Latham picked up his phone and punched in two numbers. "Would you ask Officer Nelson to step into my office. Thank you."

A few minutes later, a female officer appeared at the door.

"Here she is. Detective Perry, this is Officer Jennifer Nelson. Officer Nelson, Detective Perry needs to be driven to the Williams Auction House to serve a warrant."

"I'd be glad to help, sir," she said. Turning to Nathan, "If you're ready, we can go now."

Nathan took the warrant from the chief and turned to Nelson. "Lead the way." He was very taken with her; tall, and slender, with short brown hair.

They walked out of the office and to her police car. "The auction house isn't far from here." She pulled out into traffic.

"How long have you been a police officer?" Nathan asked.

"A little over five years. How about you?"

"I was an Army MP for five years, then worked three years as a Special Agent for the Army Criminal Investigative Command. I've been with the Mystic PD for around a year now."

"That's some good experience." She was distracted by something on the street, and picked up the microphone. "Dispatch, this is 22-03. I just spotted Neil Sandell at the corner of Dean and Broadway. I'm on another detail, could you send a unit to that location?"

"Roger, 22-03. We'll have someone en route."

"What did you see?" Nathan asked.

"He's a pickpocket we've been looking for. Besides stealing from people, we think he might have witnessed a robbery that happened a couple weeks ago."

Officer Nelson turned into the lot at the Williams Auction House and parked the car. The two officers went inside.

"Welcome to the Williams Auction House. How can I help you?" the young lady behind the counter said.

Nathan stepped forward and showed her his badge. "I'm from the Mystic Police Department. We need to see Lauren Kingsbury."

The young lady looked to her left, toward an open door. "Miss Kingsbury, these officers are here to see you."

Lauren Kingsbury, dressed very sharply in a black skirt suit and high heels, stepped to the counter. "How may I help you?"

"I'm Detective Perry. I spoke with you about the Brasher Doubloon you're auctioning next month. This is the warrant you requested." He held out the paper.

She took the warrant, and read over it. "This looks to be in order. I'll bring you back." She stepped out of the reception area and opened the door for them to enter. "I didn't expect you so soon," she said, leading them to her office.

"This is a murder case, so time is of the essence."

"I understand. Please come in and sit down." Miss Kingsbury sat behind her desk and Nathan sat in front. Officer Nelson remained standing at the door. "As I recall, you need the name of the seller."

"That's correct, and any other information you can give me," Nathan said.

She began typing on her computer. "Here we go." She turned the computer so Nathan could see the screen.

"That's interesting. Could you print that page for me?"

With a click of the mouse, the printer behind her spat out the page, and she handed it to Nathan.

"Thank you. I'm also going to need take possession of that coin," he said.

"You're serious," Miss Kingsbury said.

"It's evidence now."

She picked up the phone and called a colleague. "Would you bring item 46872 to my office please?" She hung up the phone. "It'll be right here. So, you know the seller?"

"I'm afraid I do, and I've been looking all over for this coin."

"I guess I better take it off of the auction site now." She typed more on her computer until someone came into the office holding a small box. "This should be it." She opened the box, and took out the coin, which was enclosed in a plastic holder, and handed it to Nathan.

"I honestly had my doubts that I would ever see this." He took the box from her and placed the coin back in it. "Thank you very much for your cooperation. I trust that you will not alert the owner that I have possession of the coin?"

"You have my word that I will not say anything."

"Thank you." Nathan and Officer Nelson left the building, heading back to the police department.

"You can make your arrest now," Officer Nelson said.

"I'll still need more, but yes, I can make an arrest."

When they got back to the department, Nathan went in to speak to Chief Latham. He found him in his office. "I just wanted to thank you for your help with the warrant. I got what I needed, including the coin as evidence."

The chief stood. "I'm glad I could help. Just call if you need anything else, and tell Paul that he owes me."

Nathan shook his hand. "I will." He left the building and went to his car in the parking garage. Before he got in, he took out his cell phone and called Hank.

"McCoy," Hank answered.

"Hank, I've got the coin."

"Outstanding."

"I need for you and Gloria to do something for me."

"What's that?"

"I need for the two of you to go to Boston to make an arrest for me."

Nathan made it back to the Mystic Police Department later that afternoon. He was anxious to see if Gloria and Hank had made it back from Boston yet. He went to his office first to take off his coat and sit down.

He took the box with the coin inside out of his leather portfolio, and then walked toward the interrogation rooms. Rounding a corner, he saw Hank stepping out of one of the rooms.

"Did you make the arrest?"

"We did. She's in there," Hank replied. "Gloria's inside with her."

"Thanks. I wish I could have made that arrest myself, but I didn't want to take a chance on her getting tipped off and disappearing."

He stepped inside the room. Gloria sat next to the door, and seated at the table in the middle of the room was Alex Gold, manager of the coin convention where Chuck Blanton was murdered. Nathan sat down across the table from her. "Good afternoon, Miss Gold."

She didn't respond. Nathan opened the box he held, and placed the coin on the table in front of her. She looked at the coin, and then up at him.

"You told me you hadn't see this coin, but yet, you're listed as the seller of this coin at the auction house in Providence. Didn't you think we'd eventually find out?"

"You got lucky," she said.

"What happened in Chuck's room that night? Did you get pissed off that he changed his mind about selling it?"

At that moment, Hank opened the door, sticking his head in. "Nathan, I need to speak with you."

He got up, and nodded for Gloria to go with him. They stepped out into the hallway. "What's up?"

"We just received the ballistics report from the State Police on Gates' gun."

"Not a match, right?"

Hank let out a deep breath. "It was a match."

"What? How can that be? The murderer is in there," Nathan said.

Hank handed the report to Nathan. He looked over it, and then went back into the room, followed by both Gloria and Hank. Leaning on the table, he looked at Alex Gold, "You didn't do this alone."

"I want a deal," she replied.

"Gloria, go call Daniel Grant. Tell him he needs to get here immediately," Nathan ordered.

Once Daniel Grant arrived, he and Miss Gold reached an agreement, and she told them everything. Afterward, Nathan and Grant came out of the interrogation room. Gloria and Hank, who had been watching, came out of the viewing room.

"Gloria, can you go with me to Boston right now?" Nathan asked.

"I just need to make a phone call before I go," she said, and scampered off.

Nathan turned to Hank. "Can you take care of the other suspect?"

"I can." He turned and headed out.

"This should do it, I guess," Grant said.

"The rest is up to you now. I'll call you tomorrow," Nathan said.

Grant left and Nathan went to his office. It had been a long, rough investigation, and he was so glad it was coming to an end.

"I'm ready," Gloria stood at his office door.

"Let's go."

It was late by the time all of the officers returned to Mystic with their suspects. Nathan entered the interrogation room and sat down across the table from Sarah Blanton. "We know everything, Sarah. Do you have anything to say?"

"I hated him. He was never home, and spent all of our money on those stupid coins. I went with him to a show in Boston and met Alex in a bar there. She told me about a coin Chuck said he had, but never saw. One night when he was passed out at his desk, I saw it in his hand, and took it. The stupid ass thought he lost it. I saw him looking all over the floor for it."

"Why didn't you just let him sell it? It was a priceless

coin," Nathan asked.

"He wouldn't have given me any of it. He'd have used it to buy more coins. He didn't have the nerve to tell Alex he lost it, so he told her he'd changed his mind. She was furious because she already had people interested in it. When I told her I had the coin, but didn't want Chuck to know, we came up with the plan to kill him. We just needed a way to do it."

"So, you took Bruce's gun?"

"He didn't have a clue. I took it, and put it back before he knew it was gone."

"But, what about the life insurance policy? How did that play into your scheme?" Nathan asked.

"That was a happy accident. Chuck was over-weight and not healthy at all. I knew someday he'd drop dead, and I'd be left with just that measly little policy he had through work. It wasn't enough to live on. Bruce said he had a relative that sold life insurance and we could get a policy on Chuck without him ever knowing."

"Well Sarah, you were right, Chuck never did know, but you're never going to see a penny of that money." Nathan left the room.

Out in the hallway, Hank stepped out of the viewing room with Bruce Gates.

"Mr. Gates, you saw her statement?" Nathan said.

"I was really stupid. I never knew she had my gun."

"I believe you. You won't be implicated in the murder, but there is still the little problem about the life insurance money."

"I understand. I'm willing to cooperate with you in every way possible," Gates said.

"Good."

Gates left with Hank, and Nathan went to his office. He sat down looking out the window. The sun had long set, and with no moon, it was very dark outside. It was finally over. His original suspicion of Mrs. Blanton being involved proved to be right.

His cell phone rang. He looked at the screen. Swiping, he answered. "Hello, Katherine."

"I hope you're not busy."

"I'm still at work, but just finishing up before heading home. What do you need?"

"Nothing really. I just finished bathing Simon and putting him to bed. He's looking more like you every day. When are you going to come visit?"

"How about I take off Friday and fly down for the weekend?" he asked.

"That would be great. Call me when you know your arrival time."

"I will. See you soon."

About the Author

Carol Preflatish knew at an early age that she loved to write. In high school and college, her favorite classes were composition and creative writing. But it wasn't until later in life that she decided to pursue it seriously. She published her first romantic suspense in 2009, and followed that up with six more. In 2019, Carol decided to switch to writing mysteries, with the first book in her new series, "Homecoming to Murder," releasing in March, 2020. She's a member of the national Sisters in Crime writers' organization and active in the Louisville, Kentucky Sisters in Crime chapter. Carol resides in southern Indiana.

Visit Carol's official web site at CarolPre.com

www.ingramcontent.com/pod-product-compliance
Lightning Source LLC
Chambersburg PA
CBHW030119260626
47156CB00008B/2713